# A MEETING OF CONSEQUENCE

# JOHN RYLAND

This is a work of fiction. Names, characters, places, and incidents are products of the author's imagination or are used fictitiously and are not to be construed as real. Any resemblance to actual events, locations, organizations, or persons, living or dead, is entirely coincidental.

**World Castle Publishing, LLC**
Pensacola, Florida
Copyright © 2025 John Ryland
Hardback ISBN: 9798264341397
Paperback ISBN: 9798891264670
eBook ISBN: 9798891264687
First Edition World Castle Publishing, LLC, October 6, 2025
http://www.worldcastlepublishing.com
**Licensing Notes**
Cover: Cover Designs by Karen
Editor: Karen Fuller

*In the one, there are many.*
*Of the many, there is but one.*
*Within days there are years*
*Until the hours number none.*

# CHAPTER ONE

Carver Willis sat on the edge of his bed and retrieved his wristwatch from the nightstand. It was a beautiful timepiece, a Rolex Submariner. Pre-owned, but no one else knew that. He'd bought it for himself on the tenth anniversary of hanging out his shingle.

He fogged the crystal with his breath and cleaned it on the cuff of his starched, white dress shirt. Smiling, he admired the sleek design. It was the epitome of careful craftsmanship, precision, overachievement. There were easier ways to make a watch, but this one was crafted in a way as to despite ease and simplicity. It was elegant because the makers wanted it to be elegant.

The watch was a symbol of his success. Some people hated lawyers like him. Ambulance chaser, they called him. He didn't care. He'd been making over six figures a year for a long time now. That put him in some lofty company in a piss-ant suburb like Druid Hills.

His office was a twenty-minute drive away in Souls Harbor, but it wasn't a bad commute. Having inherited his parents' home after his mother died and his father moved into assisted living, it made financial sense to stay. No sense in paying the higher property taxes if he could avoid it. Besides, County Road 14, running along the western bank of the Black Warrior River, was a scenic drive and a good way to wind down after work.

A body in the bed behind him stirred, pulling his attention from the watch. He looked over his shoulder at the form beneath the covers and smiled. Long blonde hair spilled onto the pillow next to his. Belinda Marcum was no supermodel, but she was attractive in her own way. She had a great body and took care of herself. She also never pressured him to take their relationship to the "next level," and for that, he was thankful. He'd tried that once before, and it didn't work out well.

He put his hand on the blanket covering her hip. "Don't sleep too late," he said. "I'll be leaving in about—" he looked at the watch in his hand, " —forty-five minutes."

Belinda moaned, and a long, slender arm slipped from beneath the covers, finding his hand. "Can't I stay? I'm off today."

"You know the answer, so why even ask?"

She grunted in protest as she rolled over to face him. "C'mon. We've been dating for months. Don't you trust me? It's not like I'm going to steal the candlesticks or anything."

Carver looked at her. Frustration rose in his chest. He wouldn't call what they did "dating". Once or twice a week, she'd come over, they'd drink enough to loosen her inhibitions, and they'd screw until he was done. To him, letting her sleep over was only a concession to get her to stay so late.

"Fine," she said, conceding to his stare. Her hand moved from his and slid toward his crotch. "You could stay in bed with me. You never know what might happen."

Carver smiled again as he removed her hand from his black slacks. "After last night, you'd need a hot shower," he said with an impish grin. "Besides, I've got a lot of clients to see today." He stood and smoothed the front of his shirt. "A little cooperation would be nice, you know." He turned and left the bedroom without looking back.

———

Carver flipped the switch, and a decorative fluorescent light flickered to life, illuminating the kitchen he'd remodeled after his parents' departure. Crossing the room to a deep, rich oak table, he hung his suit coat on the back of a chair. He switched on the pre-loaded coffee pot before going to the fridge. He removed two eggs from the door and went back to the stove. The sleek gas burners replaced the spiral electric ones his mother had cooked so many meals on. He didn't use them as much as she used hers, but he had them when he needed them. His mother had fed a family of three on the old meadow gold-colored appliance. He had no such aspirations.

Most things in his life, including the woman upstairs in his bed, served one of two purposes. One was to be there when he wanted them. The other was to help him make money. Appearances were important in his business. Sometimes, they were all that mattered.

Carver Willis fried his eggs over medium while he waited for the toast to pop up. When it did, he carefully scooped the eggs up and made a sandwich, breaking the yolks with the edge of his spatula. He enjoyed his sandwich and cup of black coffee over the sink, careful not to stain his shirt.

While he chewed, his eyes washed over the counter and into the living room. The old Ponderosa pine and dark shag carpet of his youth had given way to a modern design. A black leather sofa anchored the space while a small fireplace with new gas logs sat dark in the corner. His eyes roved over the sleek lines of the glass and black metal coffee table. He liked clean edges. They set boundaries. This is where one thing stopped, and another began. Boundaries were important. Boundaries were everything.

His eyes lifted to the ceiling as the sound of footsteps filtered down from the upstairs bedroom. Belinda was up. Good. She only had — he looked at his watch — fifteen minutes. He closed his eyes and sighed. She'd better not make him late. Again.

———

"Okay. Okay. Good lord, Carver," Belinda complained as he hurried her toward the door leading to the garage. "Why do you worry so much about being late? You're the freaking boss for crying out loud."

"I am the one who sets the standard, Belinda. If I drag in whenever I want, so will everyone else. I've explained that a hundred times." He opened the door and waved her out.

"You know, sometimes you can be a real jerk."

"You've said that before. You know how things are. You didn't have to come over, you know." Carver followed her into the garage, where a ten-year-old Honda Accord awaited her. Her car was next to his black Mercedes, half the age of her car.

"Maybe next time I won't," she said defiantly as she opened the driver's side door to her car and tossed an overnight bag in. "You ever consider that?"

Carver looked at her blankly. "Then I suppose I'd spend the night alone, and I wouldn't be late the next day."

"Asshole," she shot as she slid in behind the wheel and started the car. "Have a great friggin' day."

Carver hit the button to open both garage doors with one hand and looked at the watch on his other. "You too." He watched her back out, then strode to his Mercedes.

He was almost ten minutes late. If traffic wasn't bad on the highway, he could make most of that up. The road had several tight turns, but the horsepower of the Mercedes would let him get around any slowpokes with ease.

Getting in, he started the car. The engine roared to life, igniting the instrument panel before him. He revved the engine slightly, enjoying the power at his beck and call. "Damn," he said with an impish grin. "I do love this car."

Backing out of the garage, he pointed the car north and started out of the neighborhood. Resisting the urge to call the car's power into play, he moved patiently between the rows of houses.

Most of the homes were mid-century modern. Still owned by their original occupants, many of them hadn't been renovated and thus clung to their original look. A few had, however, giving him hope that in the next few years, the neighborhood would undergo a positive transformation.

As he drew even with a split-level ranch, the front door opened. He watched the elderly woman remove the large wooden four-leaf clover from a hook on the door. She wasn't wasting much time getting past yesterday's holiday. Dressed in a gray housecoat, she spared him a cursory nod as she tucked the oversized clover beneath one scrawny arm and closed the door with the other.

Carver vaguely remembered her from his youth. Maybe his parents played cards with her and her husband. Her name was Carrol something. Or was it something Carrol?

———

When he reached County Road 14, he spared a glance over his left shoulder and pulled out. His foot sank on the gas pedal, and the car accelerated quickly.

It was a beautiful spring day. Crisp and cool. The sun was out. The road was dry. He'd easily be able to make up for the time lost to Belinda's laziness.

His fingertip pressed the first button of the preset radio channels, and a deep soothing voice filled the car. Brian Sandel would give him all the latest news as he sped toward work.

Tall pines passed quickly on the right side of the car. In the breaks between them, his eyes darted to the river beyond. The water was up slightly due to last week's heavy rain. Amid the debris dislodged from feeder streams, a white jug floated gently on the current.

His eyes narrowed as he looked at it, finding it odd though he didn't know why. As a kid, he'd seen men use them as floats for night fishing. He was still wondering if the jug had a catfish on it as he turned back to the road.

"Dammit," Carver growled. He slowed quickly, watching the brake lights of the battered pick-up truck ahead of him come on. The Mercedes purred beneath him, awaiting its time to leap forward and pass.

Carver followed the man through an 'S' curve, inching closer to the rear bumper of the truck while he complained under his breath. "Who even drives fifty miles an hour?"

Coming out of the curve, he moved over slightly, allowing him a view of the road before them. Finding it clear, his foot slammed on the accelerator. The engine roared to life and moved the car into the oncoming lane. As he sped past the truck, he stole a glance at the driver.

He was an older man, probably in his early seventies. Gray stubble clung to his sunken cheeks. He turned and looked back at Carver. The scowl on his face relayed the fact that he wasn't happy.

Moving past the truck, Carver rolled his eyes and slid into the lane in front of him. "The Old Guy," as he'd named the driver, was a regular on the road. The man's schedule was slightly behind his own because he only saw him on days when Belinda made him late. Carver had passed him many times at various spots along the road, and neither time did the man look happy about it.

He's just jealous and resentful, Carver thought. The guy had probably spent his whole adult life at the same insipid job, toiling through some unskilled day only to return home to a grumpy-assed wife who licked Cheetos dust from her fingers and griped at him all evening. Old fucker.

———

Carver slowed at the intersection of County Road 14 and U.S. Highway 11. At the stop sign ahead, he'd turn right and be at the office in under five minutes. Unfortunately, he was five cars back.

He sighed, cursing Belinda again for making him late. When he was on time, there were never more than one or two cars ahead of him. Every one of these people was probably a slowpoke.

To make matters worse, traffic on the highway was thicker than normal. He pursed his lips, shaking his head resentfully as he watched the steady line of vehicles move past the intersection.

Taking the opportunity, Carver checked his hair in the

rearview mirror. Dark brown and neatly parted from left to right, nothing was out of place. He leaned forward and tilted his head back, inspecting his nostrils to make sure he didn't have any "bats in the cave". All clear, he settled into his seat for the wait.

Drumming his fingers on the steering wheel, he listened as Brian Sandel talked about a pending economic crisis. It didn't worry him much. He didn't have a ton of money in stocks. Most of his money was in secure markets, a lesson learned from his ultra-conservative father.

As a young man, he'd thought his father a fool for not taking more risks to earn greater returns. Now, as an adult, he was more prudent. It was his own money now, and the old man had started to make more sense.

*Don't let other people gamble with your money, son.*

Carver inched forward again as another car made it onto the highway. The blue sedan in front of him was leaving more space between it and the preceding car than he liked, but his crowding didn't seem to be helping.

Movement in his rearview mirror caught his attention, and Carver looked up. The beat-up truck had caught up with him and was rolling to a stop just behind his Mercedes. Damn, he thought. The guy was probably drawing some satisfaction knowing that Carver's fancy car hadn't gotten him any further along the road than his old truck had.

Anger rose in Carver's chest. Traffic sucked. He hated the stupidity of it and the waste of his time, but more than anything, he hated the fact that it was often the great equalizer. He inched closer to the blue sedan in front of him. When the sedan inched forward, he closed the gap.

His eyes watched the steady stream of traffic. A white sedan. A blue truck, another white car. Two SUVs, each a different shade of gray. His shoulders drooped, and he closed his eyes, trying to stay calm by telling himself there was nothing he could do about his place in line.

He reminded himself that he had plenty of time. Despite his complaints to Belinda, he wouldn't be late. Even with traffic, he'd just be less early than he liked. He sighed, a pang of guilt washing over him for the way he'd treated her this morning. One of these days, she was going to get sick of his shit and leave for good.

A short beep from behind opened his eyes. The first thing he saw was that the car in front of him had gone, leaving him short of the stop sign. The second thing was the man in the pick-up behind him, tossing his hands into the air impatiently. Carver snarled into his rearview mirror and rolled up to the intersection.

A quick look over his left shoulder told him he'd have time to go if he hurried. He barely stopped rolling before his foot was pressing on the accelerator again. The Mercedes leaped forward, and he was on the highway. A black SUV braked hard behind him, offering the blast of a horn as a rebuke. Carver barely noticed. He was on a mission. Every car he passed would gain him time.

———

The bridge crossing the Black Warrior River split on the eastern side. The eastbound traffic adjoined a flyover that bent to Carver's right, then back left in a long, sweeping turn. The flyovers, extending well past the banks of the river, spared traffic the chore of slogging through a low-end residential neighborhood near the river.

The bridge delivered traffic into the town of Souls Harbor from the west. He lifted his foot only slightly as the Mercedes descended the curve, his eyes looking ahead to see if the light was green. The fact that he'd managed to pass three people had only lifted his spirits slightly.

The main thoroughfare through town fanned out to four lanes after the bridge, thinning traffic. If he made the first light, he could make all of them until he had to turn. That would save him even more time.

The light was turning yellow as he made the bottom of the hill, but he stomped the gas. His car roared through the intersection just as the signal turned red. He'd made it. Looking in his rearview mirror with a smile, he watched the slowpokes come to a stop at the light. Serves you right, he thought.

His eyes came back to the road just as the traffic light ahead turned yellow. The brake lights of a crème-colored Impala, probably built in the late seventies, flashed in front of him came on. He darted into the left lane and again pressed the accelerator. He made the second light before it turned red. Barely.

Downtown Souls Harbor was a mix of old-school charm and new buildings that were constructed to match the aesthetic. One of the older buildings, a three-story brick structure painted dark green and edged in white, lumbered in the middle of the block. In its day, it had been office buildings with a bar on the bottom floor. Now, however, it had been vacant for at least ten years, and it showed.

In front of the building, a wide set of concrete steps led to the sidewalk, breaking up the rows of windows. Beside the steps, a man leaned against the chipped paint of the bricks. He had a cigarette clutched between the pointer and middle fingers of his right hand, which hung by his side. A thin tendril of smoke rose lazily from the ember. The man wore a suit that fit him well, charcoal gray with a burgundy shirt. His tie was dark, with a design that matched the color of his shirt.

As Carver drew even with him, the man puckered his lips and blew a plume of smoke in his direction. Behind the smoke, he grinned, and he threw Carver a quick wink.

Carver spared a look over his shoulder as he passed the man, discovering him watching intently. A shudder ran down Carver's spine as he turned back to the traffic in front of him. Unnerved by the strange feeling that he knew the man but didn't want to, he'd slowed down and was in danger of not making the next light.

He grunted and changed lanes. Finding an opening, then throttled up the Mercedes' engine. The light turned red before he reached it, but he was too close to stop. In the back of his mind, he thought about the fact that people were usually slow off the light. He should clear the intersection before the cross traffic caught him.

He entered the intersection at the same time as a silver car. His eyes widened, and he drew in a sharp breath. His foot moved to the brake, but it was too late. Carver gripped the steering wheel, his body tensing. "Son of a—" was all he had time to say before everything went black.

# CHAPTER TWO

Two slender arms wrapped around Benjamin Howard's neck from behind as he sat shirtless at the kitchen table. He was making his way through his third cup of coffee and contemplating his future, something he'd done too much of lately.

"You're up early."

"Hmm," he said, a hand coming up to caress the arm laying across his chest. "Got that job interview today. Eight o'clock."

"The one with the construction company?" Angie Howard, his wife of seven years, slid her hands across his smooth chest as she rose from Bennie's back. "Dad says that's a big outfit," she told him, moving toward the coffee pot. "They're always needing help."

"Yeah," Benny said with a quiet sigh. Construction wasn't his first choice, but nobody else wanted a middle-aged, failed rock guitarist.

When his band, Midnight Blue, broke up, he spent the next few months trying to piece it back together. After that, he played solo gigs around town when he could get them, but he was no singer. Not a lead anyway. He played guitar and sang backup. That was his thing. They were the only skills that he had, and right now there wasn't a market for either.

After months of surviving on Angie's income as an X-ray tech, things were getting lean. Subconsciously, he'd come to the decision before she'd sat him down and had the talk with him. Angie was a loving, supportive wife, but she was also a realist. She paid the bills every month. She didn't have the option of pretending that they weren't in dire straits like him. Still, he knew.

Six months after the band's break-up, they were into their

savings. Not that they ever had much to begin with. A month after that, off-brand foods started showing up in the pantry. Happy Hills sweet corn replaced Delmonte. Crème Delights replaced the Oreos. One by one, they disappeared until everything on the shelves was different. Lesser. Cheaper. A few months after that, the snacks went away altogether. Angie said she was on a diet and didn't want the temptation, but he knew she was sparing him further shame.

It was raining the night of "the talk," as he came to think of it. He'd returned late from a gig with fifty bucks in his pocket. It wasn't much, but it was something. Tonight, he wouldn't feel like as much of a loser. He was contributing something.

She was still in the compulsory pale green scrubs that her department wore. She had worked a double shift. They could use the extra cash. There was rent, the light bill. Their phones. Gas wasn't getting any cheaper, you know.

"I know you're trying. I really do."

The look on her face told him it hurt her to ask him to give up on his dream. It said that she knew he was talented, but also that they were circling the drain. She took his hands in hers. Her fingertips found the callous on his right thumb, the one he sometimes used to strum. It was the callous he'd worn on it playing "Angie" by the Rolling Stones over and over one night when they were dating. They drank whiskey and Coke, and he sat on the trunk of her car and played all night for her.

"But we really need some more money coming in. Things are bad, Bennie. I can't do it by myself anymore. It's just for a little while. Until we get things caught back up."

The pain in his chest was like a stab wound. Losing the band had hurt. Not being able to find steady work had hurt. But the single tear that escaped her blue eye and rolled down her cheek had nearly killed him.

He went out the next morning and started looking for a "real job". Of course, he didn't have any real skills outside of the music industry. After a week of rejections, he cut his hair to shoulder length, hoping a change in appearance might make him more hirable. Six inches of his life fell to the bathroom floor at Angie's feet.

When she allowed him to look in the mirror, he feigned an appreciation for it. Said it was much cooler on his neck, that it would be easier to keep up now. Inside, though, he was dying. Cutting his hair was more symbolic than anything else. If he got a call tomorrow, he could pick up with just about anybody, and his hair wouldn't make a difference. One call from one band was all he needed. That's all it would take. One break and he'd be on top. But he knew the call wouldn't come.

When she left him alone to clean up his hair, he knelt and pushed it into a pile with his fingertips. Gently. Shaking his head, he looked at it. It was over. He'd never be famous. He'd never get to play before a packed house of adoring fans. Now he was just another former guitar player.

The loose hair slipped over his fingertips and into the toilet. He stared at it, watching it float on the water. A hand found the lever and flushed it. His eyes followed the sandy brown strands as they circled the drain, like their finances.

The hair clumped together as it neared the drain, then disappeared in one gurgling heap. They were gone.

When the water level began to rise in the bowl, his eyes grew wide. "No, no, no," he begged, watching the level grow higher. He jiggled the handle, but the water kept rising in the bowl. "Shit. Angie!"

She appeared in the doorway, flour-covered hands raised in front of her like a surgeon. "What?" Her eyes followed his to the toilet, and she gasped. "What did you do?"

"I flushed it," Bennie said, panic rising in his voice.

"Grab the plunger," she said, grabbing a towel to clean her hands. "Hurry before it overflows."

Benny grabbed the plunger, shoving it into the bowl. He

pushed it into the drain and began working it up and down, stopping every few strokes to see if it worked. The water was near the rim when the clog finally gave way.

"Jesus," he said, falling against the wall. "Talk about adding insult to injury."

"Aw," Angie said. Her shoulders dropped and her head fell to one side. "I thought you said you liked it shorter."

"I do," he lied, forcing a smile. He pushed a hand through his hair. "It'll just take some getting used to."

"Well," she bent forward and kissed his lips. "I'd think you were the best-looking guy in the room even if you were bald."

Benny smiled. "Let's not go that far, but thanks." He slipped his arms around her waist. "I love you."

"I love you too," she said, hugging him. Pulling away, she draped the towel over his shoulder. She grinned, shaking her head. "Just toss the rest in the trash when you sweep up, okay?"

―――――

"Everything okay?" Angie asked, a curious look on her face as she joined him at the table with her own cup of coffee.

"Uh, yeah. Just thinking."

"Thinking? You have been up a while." She sipped from her cup and moaned. "I can barely think 'till I'm at least a half cup in."

Bennie smiled, but it was half-hearted, drawing a quizzical look from his wife.

"Are you nervous about the interview?"

Bennie shrugged. "I guess. A little. I don't know."

She extended a hand, putting it on his arm. "I know it's not what you want, sweetie. I really do. And I appreciate the hell out of you for doing this." When his response came in the form of another shrug, she continued. "Maybe it'll just be temporary. For the summer, you know. We'll save up, and in the fall you can look again. Maybe you'll get a call, catch on with someone big."

"That's doubtful," he said.

"Oh sweetie, don't let this get you down. It'll get better. I promise."

"Wouldn't it have to?" he asked, unable to look at her. His thumb ran up and down the handle of his cup. "Thank you for not giving me hell about all this."

"About what?"

"About being such a loser."

"Benjamin Howard, you are not a loser. I know that for a fact because I'm awesome and I'd never be married to a loser." Angie laughed, shaking his arm. "C'mon. It's a new day. Who knows, today might be the best day ever."

"Maybe so," he said. It was doubtful, but he didn't want to ruin her mood. "I gotta meet this dude at eight."

"That's fine. You can drop me off just before seven, and you'll have plenty of time to make it across town." She drank from her coffee and stood. "Now, what do you want for breakfast? I'm going to send my man off with a full belly for his first day on the job."

"I haven't even interviewed yet."

"It doesn't matter. I got a good feeling. How can they not love you?"

"Because I don't know my butt from a hole in the ground when it comes to construction?"

"You've done plenty of things around here. Did you put that on your resume?"

"There wasn't a line on the application for hanging shelves and changing light bulbs, Ang."

"Doesn't matter," she said as she retrieved pans from the cupboard. She pointed a skillet at him, "You'll get the job. You're a hard worker and a good man. Surely, they'll see that right off the bat."

Bennie sighed and sipped his coffee, hoping that they would. Being rejected for paying gigs was one thing; being rejected for a minimum wage job might be more than he could take.

———

"This is good."

Bennie pulled his wife's silver Toyota Camry to the curb near the back entrance of Souls Harbor General. "Love you, babe."

"Love you too." Angie leaned over, accepting his kiss as she gathered her things. "Good luck today." She held up two crossed fingers on one hand while she opened the door with her other. "You got this."

Bennie smiled, watching her get out of the car. "Thanks, babe. Hope you have a good day."

"Bennie," she said, bending to look back into the car. "I do love you, and I do appreciate everything you do for me. For us."

Bennie smiled. "Right back at you, babe. Right back at you."

Angie stabbed a finger at him. "You got this."

Bennie opened his mouth to respond, but she slammed the door and grabbed her security badge as she headed for the sliding doors to the hospital.

He sighed and picked up his phone. Angie had loaded the address of the construction office in the navigation app on his phone; now all he had to do was follow the blue line. The office was across town in the industrial park. He didn't even know what an industrial park was or that they had one.

As he pulled away from the curb, his mind conjured images of metal buildings with high smokestacks billowing clouds of black soot into the air, and he groaned. The image in his head was more fitting in a Pink Floyd video than in Souls Harbor, Alabama. Hell, he thought. Maybe it's right, though. The only thing he knew for sure was that he didn't have a clue.

Rolling slowly through the parking lot, Bennie switched on the radio. He was instantly met by a sappy pop song on the channel Angie loved. He fingered his way through the channels until he landed on one that he liked, catching the middle of "I've got a feeling" from the Black-Eyed Peas. It was a little too "Pop" for the band to play, but Angie loved it, and he liked the beat.

"Cool," he said, his fingers strumming the steering wheel, following along on the guitar chords. He had plenty of time to get across town, even with rush hour traffic building. He decided to take his time, find the place, then chill in the car until his appointment. He'd take the time to psyche himself up so that he could hide his disappointment. If he got the job, he'd bring home just under three hundred bucks a week, after taxes. It wasn't a lot, but anything would help.

Leaving the hospital campus, he turned onto an already crowded feeder road. He moaned, shaking his head, baffled by the sheer number of cars on the road. He hadn't seen early morning traffic in years. His days consisted of sleeping late, getting up, and slowly preparing himself for whatever gig they had that night.

While waiting at the traffic light, he decided that he'd play his guitar tonight. He needed to keep his fingers loose, just in case. But even if nobody ever called, he enjoyed playing and hadn't done enough of it lately. He'd take this crummy job if they offered, but he wouldn't like it. He owed it to Angie to pull his own weight with the bills. He'd hammer and nail or carry wood or whatever they told him to, but he'd never quit playing. He'd rather die first.

Bennie settled into the seat, moving his head to the rhythm of the music, though his thoughts were far away. Maybe things wouldn't be so bad. Maybe this respite from playing gigs would give him a new appreciation for the life he had and a new hunger to get it back. He might even finish some of the original songs he'd been working on.

———

Bennie picked up his phone from the passenger seat and stared at the blue navigation line in disbelief. He still had a couple of miles to go, and time was coming up against him. He'd made it through most of town without much delay, but utility work downtown had bottlenecked traffic.

Before him, cars jostled for position, inching forward at an agonizingly slow pace. Somewhere behind him and to the left, a horn beeped as one of the many impatient drivers spoke up. He drew in a deep breath and let it out slowly. Pushing a hand through his hair, he looked around.

The passenger in a white Yukon, a woman with blond hair who looked to be in her mid-thirties, was looking at him. When she caught his eye, she offered a quick smile, then turned away. Bennie chuckled, shaking his head. He'd never had a problem with the ladies. Every night, after their show, he could have had his pick, but always declined. Angie was his girl, plain and simple.

When the Yukon moved forward, he noticed her watching him in the side mirror. He wiggled his fingers above the steering wheel and gave her a head nod. She wasn't unattractive, which left him wondering about the male driver. Was the guy her husband? A boyfriend? Maybe they just carpooled.

With the distraction of the woman moving ever so slowly forward while he sat still, Bennie looked at his phone again. The tiny triangle on the blue line was in the same place it had been for the last ten minutes. He was trapped in the middle of the block with five cars ahead of him waiting to merge. He sighed and dropped the phone back onto the seat.

"C'mon," he groaned in a loud whisper. Who thought utility work in the middle of town during rush hour was a good idea?

Ahead of him, the cars in his lane began to move. Bennie sat up in his seat, revived by the sight of workmen now collecting on the sidewalk. As he rolled up, he saw four men wrestling an odd-looking machine over the curb. Long wires that might have been fiberoptic cables stuck out of the end facing him.

He had no idea what the colors of the cables meant, but it seemed important that the workers keep them in order. The man in the white hat was pointing to the five cables with enthusiasm and shouting at the men beside the machine. There were three green wires, a silver one, and a black one.

As he drew closer, everything slowed. One of the workers turned and stared directly at him. He was of average height and thinly built. Blonde hair hung from beneath the grimy orange hard hat on his head, landing between the shoulders of the dingy white t-shirt he wore. A cigarette dangled limply from the corner of his mouth.

His eyes met Bennie's, and he nodded, offering a crooked smile. Rolling past the man, Bennie couldn't escape the feeling that he knew the guy from somewhere. There was a familiarity to him, but when the worker gave him a wink, a chill ran down his spine.

The honk of an impatient driver behind him yanked Bennie from his malaise. He shook his head and moved up, quickly closing the gap on the car in front of him. The red sedan scurried across the intersection, but the light caught Benny.

As soon as he stopped, his eyes darted to the passenger side mirror. The man was still standing on the sidewalk, his chore left to the other workers. His eyes were locked on Bennie's car. On him. The man's gaze had a weight to it that Bennie could feel in his chest. It was as if the man knew a secret that was about to be revealed.

Unsettled, Bennie looked away. The road in front of him was the main thoroughfare in town. Four lanes of traffic passed quickly. Each car made a "shoop" sound as it passed, the wind buffeting Angie's Camry ever so slightly.

Disoriented, Bennie shook his head. The world in front of him was progressing at normal speed, but the world around him was still in slow motion.

His hand retrieved the phone, and he checked his progress.

The marker representing his car hadn't moved much, but his eyes were drawn to the blue line he'd been following. It progressed forward from his position only slightly and ended suddenly.

Bennie looked up, his jaw hanging open. He estimated that the end of the blue line would put him directly in the middle of the intersection.

He grunted in frustration and shook his phone. "Piece of junk," he whispered to the empty car. "Great." He dropped the phone back onto the seat with a sigh and shook his head.

Though he didn't want them to, his eyes went back to the mirror. The man was still standing where he'd been, but now had one hand in the pocket of his jeans. The other rose to the cigarette clenched in his lips. Pinching it between his fingers, he took a deep drag before withdrawing it. The paper on the butt stuck to his dry lip, tugging at it gently.

The stranger puckered his lips, creating lines in the pale skin. A plume of smoke erupted from his lips, aimed straight at Bennie. Then, he thumped the butt right at his car.

Bennie's head jerked around just as the light was changing from red to green. Eager to be rid of the peculiar stranger, he stomped the gas pedal. Angie's Camry responded immediately, propelling him into the intersection.

There was a flash of movement, black like a shadow, then the unmistakable sound of squealing tires. Bennie looked to his left, but the window was full of a shiny chrome grill. The morning sun glinted off the steel. His body tensed. "Sh—" was all he had time to get out before a dark silence enveloped him.

# CHAPTER THREE

Carver Willis stood from the bed and stretched his back while he yawned. He turned back and looked at the woman sleeping on the pillow next to his. The hint of a smile came to his lips. He didn't allow her to stay over a lot, especially during the week, but she'd been very appreciative of the gesture.

"Hey, sleepyhead. Wake up. You know I hate to be late."

A mumbled reply escaped the covers.

"Don't make me late again, Belinda. I'm serious. C'mon. Get up."

Another mumbled reply, louder this time in protest.

Turning from the bed, he rubbed the sleep from his eyes with a fist as he headed for the bathroom. He showered every morning, but after last night, he felt like he needed a long one. He wasn't getting any younger, and as he drew closer to fifty, his body and his doctor were both telling him to slow down. Of course, he refused to listen.

Nobody told Carver Willis what to do.

In the bathroom, he turned on the shower and went to the toilet. Leaning in with one hand on the wall, he relieved himself. "Belinda," he called through the open door. He didn't expect a reply and didn't get one. He rolled his eyes and got into the shower.

The water was hot. Carver stood in the stream and let it hit him in the face for a long time. He took a deep breath through his nose, letting the steam open his sinuses.

Now fully awake, he grabbed his shampoo and went to work on his morning routine. Shampoo, conditioner, face scrub, then body wash. In his line of work, appearances mattered. He was competing with younger lawyers who flaunted prestigious degrees from universities that he couldn't afford and looked down on people like him. He knew what they called him, but he didn't care.

So far, he'd stayed ahead of the pack through hard work, diligence, and creative advertising. They could call him what they wanted as long as he kept going to the bank with fat checks.

Coming from average working-class parents, he couldn't rely on his father's connections to get him cases. Short of the money his father had given him to pay for his bachelor's degree, he'd built himself by himself and wasn't ready to give that up just yet.

He could still chew up any two-bit kid the insurance companies threw at him and could work an aging judge like a piece of soft clay. His reputation as a pit bull in the courtroom led to a lot of settlements, which was fine with him.

Carver shut off the water and grabbed a towel. Stepping out of the shower, he wrapped it around his waist and went to the sink.

"Belinda, wake up. C'mon." He turned back to the steamed-covered mirror, shaking his head. He leaned in to wipe it, but hesitated. He stood, one hand hovering inches from the glass, his eyes locked on the distorted reflection.

The thin veil of condensation skewed his features, making him look like someone else. His head tilted to one side. His eyes narrowed. The reflection reminded him of someone he knew or had met, but when his mind shuffled through his recent clients, he came up dry.

Curious, he leaned closer. Some of the fog had cleared, affording him a slightly better view. The hair in the reflection seemed to be neatly combed, parted on the left, and swept to the right. Carver's hand went to the top of his head. His hair was a mess and soaking wet, yet the reflection of his hand landed on the neat hair in the mirror.

"What the hell?" he muttered. The eyes in the reflection

stared back at him, cold and distant, ignoring the hand as it dropped slowly from his head to the edge of the sink. Carver moved closer. Now, within inches of the mirror, he examined the stranger before him.

His left hand rose slowly, fingers together. When his fingertips touched the glass just above the reflection, a smile slipped across the lips. Straight white teeth gleamed through the fog. Carver gasped, withdrawing. He hadn't smiled.

Recovering, he wiped a hand across the mirror, clearing a swath directly in front of his face. He leaned back in, staring at himself. In the mirror, his hair was a mess, and he was no longer smiling.

Carver threw a glance through the open door, checking for Belinda. Finding only shadows in the bedroom, he sighed and turned back to the mirror.

"Damn," he said to his reflection. "You need some coffee."

―――――

The fluorescent light flickered to life above his head as Carver crossed the kitchen. He switched on the coffee pot and put two slices of bread in the toaster. The strange reflection in the mirror began to fade in his mind as he went about his morning routine, dismissed as an optical illusion and a light hangover.

He ate two fried eggs on toast over the sink while he drank coffee. Upstairs, feet on the floor. Belinda was up. He looked at the clock on the wall and rolled his eyes, remembering why he tried to avoid letting her stay over during the week.

When the sound of the shower filtered down to him, his mind began to conjure images of her body. She wasn't heavy, but she was thick. Stout. There was a fullness to her hips that he liked. She also had a nice rack and a great ass.

He considered joining her, but the clock was glaring down at him from its perch above the door. He shook his head, chased the thoughts away, and finished his coffee. A busy day awaited him.

———

"Belinda," he called as he topped the stairs. "C'mon. It's time to go." He strode through the bedroom as the water shut off, making the open bathroom door just as she was stepping out of the shower.

"Damn," he said, his impatience pushed aside by the sight of her nakedness.

She smiled at him, holding her hands out to the side as she posed for him. "Like what you see?"

"That I do. Yes," he said, nodding. "Unfortunately, we don't have time for anything fun." He pushed up the sleeve of his dress shirt and showed her his watch. "It's getting late."

"You know," she said, putting one foot on the toilet as she toweled her leg, "If you just let me stay, you wouldn't have to worry about all that."

Carver sighed. "Let's not get into that now, okay?"

"I'm just saying," she went on as she switched legs. A seductive smile slipped across her lips. "Last night could be an everyday occurrence."

Carver went to her as she stood. He grabbed two handfuls of her backside and pulled her to him. "I don't know if I could handle all this every night. Now, get that beautiful ass in gear, sweetheart." Pulling away, he slapped her naked butt.

"It's not like I'd rob you. Damn, Carver."

"That's not it at all," he said as he swiped at the droplets of water on his shirt collected from Belinda's wet body. "It's just a thing that I have. You know how it is. I've told you from the beginning."

"The beginning was a long time ago, Carver. I figured we would move past that," she said, wrapping herself in the towel. She pushed past him, deliberately rubbing her breasts against his chest.

Carver watched her go, his eyes devouring the creamy skin of her thighs beneath the towel. He felt a stirring in his loins but fought it. He didn't have time. Not even for a quickie.

―――

"I mean, your office doesn't even open for like an hour and a half, Carver," Belinda protested as he ushered her through the kitchen toward the door leading to the garage.

"I know when the office opens, but Jean gets there at eight-thirty sharp, and I like to be the first one in. It sets a good example."

"Uh-huh," Belinda said, stopping at the door and turning to face him. "Maybe Jean gives you a little treat every morning," she added, grabbing his crotch.

"No," he replied, reaching around Belinda to open the door. "Jean is sixty-five and wears bifocals on a chain around her neck." He swept his hand toward the garage. "And, if you met her, you'd see that she's probably never given a blow job in her whole life."

"Sucks being her, I bet," Belinda said with a laugh. "Or rather, it doesn't suck." She laughed louder, amused at her own joke. Carver didn't laugh, but he did look at his watch and sigh.

Belinda opened the door to her car and looked back at Carver. "Has anyone ever told you that you can be an asshole sometimes?" she asked.

"Yes," he told her with a grin. "A lot of people, and I'm pretty sure one of them was you."

Belinda rolled her eyes and got into her car with a huff. "Well then, have a great freaking day."

―――

Carver's tension began to melt away as soon as he settled into the leather seat of his Mercedes. The purr of the engine enveloped him like a warm hug. He loved driving the car more than he admitted. Other than a piece of junk Chevy Chevelle, his first car, he'd never felt so connected to a vehicle.

Bright sunshine greeted him as he backed out of the garage. It was a beautiful spring morning. Blue sky stretched over the houses in his neighborhood, birds sang, and the road was dry. He'd be able to make up most of the time Belinda had cost him during the drive into town.

Rolling slowly through the neighborhood, his eyes washed over the houses. Still owned by the original tenants, many of them needed updating. As he neared a mailbox with Benyon in gold block letters, he caught sight of an elderly man standing at a workbench inside the garage.

The old man stopped what he was doing and turned to look at Carver, a screwdriver clutched in his left hand. The old man's eyes narrowed slightly, his head moving to follow Carver's black Mercedes until he was past.

Carver shook his head. "That was weird," he said with a half-hearted chuckle. Ahead of him on the left, a white truck sat in the driveway of another neighbor. The driver's door was open, and the burly man sitting behind the wheel was talking on his phone.

As Carver drew closer, the man slipped from the seat and stood, one hand resting on the silver toolbox. His eyes were locked on Carver. The hand holding the phone fell slowly until it was at his side.

Carver offered a wave and a half smile, but the man didn't return either. He stood motionless except for his head, which was following the Mercedes.

Carver's brow furrowed. The old man's stare could be expected. Old people were usually nosy and watched everything, but this felt different. The blank expression on the younger man's face had an ominous feel to it.

Eager to be rid of the odd stare, Carver pressed the accelerator, and the Mercedes surged past the driveway. He was used to people looking. The shiny black Mercedes he was driving was an eye-catcher. He'd seen it from across the lot and knew that he wanted it. But this was different. They weren't looking at his car; they were looking at him.

———

On County Road Fourteen, Carver finally switched on the radio. The voice of Brian Sandel filled the car with a deep, soothing sound, despite being in the middle of a discussion on what he called "An impending financial crisis."

The financial crisis, if it came, wouldn't affect Carver much. There would always be insurance companies, and insurance companies always had plenty of money.

A smile tugged at the corners of his mouth, remembering how proud his father was when he won his first big case. He'd taken on the insurance company for Southern Freight and Logistics after an accident with a passenger car. He'd discovered altered logbooks, an old methamphetamine habit that the driver had, and some questionable repairs to the big rig. Faced with all the evidence, they'd settled for 1.2 million.

"Thatta boy. Stick it to those damned insurance companies," the elder Willis had said. "Servs 'em right. They been sticking it to us for years."

Carver pressed the gas further, and the Mercedes accelerated. Vibrations from the powerful motor made their way through Carver's seat. He loved to feel the engine work. Immediately, muscles that he didn't know were tense began to relax.

He worked his way through an 'S' curve without slowing, the car hugging the road expertly. Carver smiled, enjoying the sensation, but it was short-lived. As he rounded the last curve, he found himself behind an older model truck. He shared his commute with several other regulars. Most of them he recognized, but neither liked nor disliked any of them. The truck now in front of him was a whole different story.

He only had to deal with the two-tone brown truck, with the darker shade on the bottom, when he was running late. He recognized it instantly as "The Old Man," as he'd named the guy. The guy never got over fifty miles per hour, no matter how close

Carver rode his ass.

Caught by a double yellow center line, Carver lifted his foot from the accelerator with a groan. Resigning himself to being stuck, at least for now, he relaxed into the leather seat. On the radio, Brian Sandel began working his way through the stock parade.

As the road neared the river, the trees thinned, allowing the morning sunlight to pour between them. The effect was a series of long, dark stripes across the road like a picket fence of shadows. Entering the stretch, the truck in front of him was struck by a second of bright sun, then shadow, creating a strobe effect. At higher speeds, it could be disorienting, but the old guy was doing his usual fifty miles per hour.

Bathed in momentary light, Carver noticed the driver turning his head to the right, as if looking over his shoulder. He squinted, losing sight of the man as he fell into shadow and his own car entered the sun. When he entered the shade and the truck entered the light, he found the old man looking back at him, his chin nearly resting on his shoulder.

The man in the truck never looked happy when Carver sped past him, but this morning, he looked particularly angry. Carver lifted his foot slightly, and the distance between them grew. The truck fell into shadow, and he squinted again as the sun fell on him. He lowered his visor, but the angle of the sun rendered it useless. He flipped it back up with a grunt.

The next time the light slipped between the trees and bathed the truck, Carver's eyes bulged. The old man's head was turned unnaturally far, almost looking directly backward. His eyes were fixed on Carver. His thin lips were pursed tightly in an angry scowl.

"Holy shit." Carver's foot rose from the accelerator, increasing the distance between them again. Unnerved, he took a deep breath and let it out slowly. How could anyone turn their head so far, let alone an old man?

Following the truck through another series of alternating shade and sun, Carver kept watch on the man's face. He never took his eyes off Carver, yet somehow maneuvered the curves perfectly.

"What the hell is wrong with everybody today?"

After an eighteen-wheeler hauling a backhoe rattled past, Carver checked the road ahead of the pickup. It was clear enough to pass. Finally. He stomped the gas pedal, and the Mercedes leaped forward. He sped past the old truck, deliberately keeping his eyes on the road ahead of him. He didn't know what he might see, but didn't want to find out.

———

Traffic was light on the bridge crossing the river, allowing Carver to work his way through the cars easily. By the time he entered the long, sweeping curve that would deliver the cars into town, he was at the front of the pack. The light turned green before he got to it. Glancing at his watch, he smiled. Despite the strange morning, he'd be at work well before Jean.

His schedule intact, Carver relaxed and let his eyes take in the downtown area. Most of the old buildings had been restored, and the new ones had been purposely built in the same style. The downtown area had a certain synergy that he'd always appreciated. There was a nice mix of businesses, from pubs to restaurants to office buildings. It was also designed to be pedestrian-friendly. A strip of grass and a wide sidewalk separated the road and the buildings, ushering people to and from their appointments.

As traffic tightened, Carver slowed. He matched the speed of the black SUV in front of him and relaxed further. He was in town, traffic was moving, and the lights in front of him were all green. A few more blocks and he'd turn left and be at his office. Five minutes, tops.

Approaching a three-story brick building on his left, Carver's eyes were drawn to the dark green paint. One of the few that hadn't been remodeled, the color stuck out like a sore thumb. The building was vacant, leaving him to assume that whoever bought it would have to repaint the exterior. He'd heard that the city was a bit of a stickler, especially with the new, younger mayor who had been elected last term. Whatever happened to it, it had to look better than the dark green color it wore now.

His eyes washed down the building, landing on a man sitting on the concrete steps at the entrance. His body sank, as if he'd suddenly gained five hundred pounds. Something changed as he approached the man. Cars sped past him in the other lanes, but for him, the world began to slow to an unnatural pace.

The man on the steps was younger than him, but not much so. His hair was neatly parted, and he wore an uneven smile. A flash of burgundy escaped the lapels of his gray suit coat. The man looked to be enjoying the cigarette in his hand, probably his last for a few hours if he worked in one of the nearby offices.

As Carver drew closer, the man lifted the cigarette. His lips tightened around it. The ember grew into a red fireball as he took a long drag. His lungs filled, spreading the lapels of his coat. A loose design of gray lines created a grid over the background of his tie, which matched his shirt.

The man looked directly at Carver. His eyes were dark, empty. He lowered the cigarette and blew smoke toward Carver as he passed. The smoke left his lips in a tight plume, extending well above the sidewalk before finally billowing into a cloud.

Carver clenched his brow and shook his head. This commute was growing odder by the minute. First the stares from his neighbors, then the old man, and now this guy. What the hell was happening to everybody?

A horn blast shook Carver from his stupor, and he looked up. He'd slowed to a crawl and was in danger of not making the next light. After a quick glance over his shoulder, he changed lanes and stepped on the gas. The signal thirty feet ahead of him was already yellow. He'd have to hurry if he was going to make it. His foot sank on the gas pedal. The car raced forward. The light turned red. He was too close to stop.

As he passed beneath the light, movement caught his eye. A silver car jumped into view, firing off the side street as soon as the signal turned green. Someone else was in a hurry.

Carver's foot instinctively moved to the brake pedal. The car's emergency stop feature engaged, blaring in his ears, but it was too late. He was too close and going too fast. His fingers gripped the steering wheel, his knuckles turning white.

"Son of a—" Carver Willis didn't get a chance to finish his sentence before the world went black.

# CHAPTER FOUR

Benjamin Howard, "Bennie" to his wife and friends, spooned sugar into his coffee. One. Two. Three. Stirring it with one hand, he wiped a few spilled granules onto the floor with the other. The cup, printed with Westbrook Baptist Church in blue letters, was a gift from a group that had passed through the neighborhood a few years back. He'd accepted the cup and the pamphlets, then told them he was busy and closed the door.

It was one of a set of "Church Cups" they'd collected over the years, each from a different church. Apparently, someone in the ministry had decided to target coffee drinkers who needed to hear the word of God. He didn't know how effective it was, but it hadn't worked on him and Angie. They were nice cups, though.

He took his coffee to the table tucked beneath a set of windows in the corner of the kitchen. The table was pushed against the wall, trapping one of the chairs. One of the others sat against the wall, holding a stack of old magazines. When they didn't eat in front of the television, they used the same two chairs. Age and use were taking a toll on them, as proven by the wobble the chair did when accepting his weight.

Sitting in a pool of light from a fixture hanging from the ceiling, he stared at the coffee in his cup. Still spinning from being stirred, a small swirl of bubbles stared back at him.

He had a job interview this morning. Some construction outfit across town. He didn't know shit about commercial construction, but they'd run an ad for "helpers and apprentices," so he'd called to apply. When a woman on the phone asked if he was applying for the helper position or the apprenticeship, he told her that he didn't know the difference. She said she'd put him down as a "helper," and he could change it later. He hadn't even shown up yet and already felt stupid.

He sipped the coffee with his right hand and set it down. Curling the fingers on his left, he looked at the calluses on the tips. He'd earned them from years of playing lead guitar for the band Midnight Blue.

For years, they'd toured a lot, mostly college towns around the south, hoping for that big break that always seemed just out of reach. Twice it looked like they were going to sign a record deal, but twice it fell through. As the years passed, things stagnated. They became old news, and fewer and fewer people came to their shows. They could still get an audience, but they couldn't pack it out like the newer, trendier bands.

Still, he persisted. Even when Marcus, their drummer, left to get a "real job" after the birth of his first child. The guy who replaced him, Ron, was almost as good as Marcus, but he didn't bring the same energy.

At their height, they made good money, but touring was expensive. Luckily, Angie got her hands on enough to help with the bills and even managed to save some. He was gone a lot, but he called her every night before their show. "We're all right," she'd tell him whenever he asked about the money. "Not rich, but the bills are paid, and you're happy. That's all that matters."

Bennie sighed. It had been a long time since she told him that they were all right. It had been a long time since things were all right. They played rock and roll, the very epitome of the 'stick it to the man' culture, yet they'd fallen victim to one of the oldest economic models there was. Supply and demand.

When Cole, the lead singer, got married, things started to go downhill. He started showing up late for rehearsal or left early, and even bailed on a show in Pascagoula, Mississippi. They'd muddled through without him and got paid, but the owner wasn't happy. They never played that club again.

One day, he walked into rehearsal and just quit. He said he was moving to Tennessee with his wife to be closer to her family. And that was that. They tried to find a replacement, but no one could agree on any one singer. Soon after that, they were just done. He brought his guitars and amps home and stuck them in a closet. The band was done.

"You're up early."

Bennie startled as two slender arms wrapped around his bare chest from behind.

"Did I scare you?" Angie asked with a quiet laugh.

Bennie shook his head. "Nah. I was just thinking. I didn't hear you coming."

Angie drug her fingers across his chest as she stood. "Are you nervous about the interview today?" she asked on her way to the coffee pot.

"I don't guess," Bennie said with a shrug. "Either they'll hire me, or they won't."

Angie looked over her shoulder at him. "You okay?"

"Yeah. I'm good."

"Look," she said as she doctored her own cup of coffee. She brought it back to the table and sat. "I know this isn't ideal."

Bennie grunted then sipped his coffee.

"But I want you to know that either way, I'm proud of you for trying."

"It's a minimum wage job, Ange. I didn't cure polio."

"Still." She reached out and laid a hand on his arm. "I know it's been tough on you since the band broke up."

Bennie shrugged one shoulder and looked out the window. It was a hard pill to swallow, but he'd done it. Although it wasn't his fault, the band had failed. It was his band. He should have pushed harder and gone after more, bigger venues. He should have been able to get them a record deal, but he couldn't.

"It is what it is," he finally said.

"Dad says this is a big outfit with lots of potential to work your way up."

From what? Helper to apprentice? "I don't really know

crap about construction if you haven't noticed."

"Don't be silly. You do lots of stuff around here that's construction-type stuff."

"Really?" he asked with a grin. "When I filled out the application online, I didn't see a space for changing lightbulbs or hanging shelves."

"Still. You're a hard worker. You'll be just fine. Give yourself a few days to catch the gist of it, and you'll do just fine."

"I hope you're right. I told them I don't have any tools, and it didn't seem to bother them."

"See," she said.

"See what?" he asked. "What kind of construction can I do without tools?"

"I'm sure they have it covered. Like I told you, Dad said it was a big company. They probably have tools just laying around the shop place or whatever it's called."

Bennie chuckled. At least someone in the world knew less about construction than he did. "Maybe so."

"You'll see. Today is going to be an awesome day. You wait and see. I got a feeling." Angie stood and shoved her hands in the front pockets of her pale green scrub top, feeling around for the things she kept there. Satisfied, she said, "I gotta pee and get my badge, but other than that I'm ready."

"Okay," Bennie said, pushing up from the table. "I'll finish getting dressed."

———

Angie spent most of the drive on her phone, scrolling through her social media accounts and sharing memes with Bennie. When they pulled up to the back of Souls Harbor General, she dropped her phone into a pocket on the front of her scrub top and retrieved her identification badge.

When she lifted the front of her shirt to clip it onto one side of the V neck, Bennie caught a glimpse of the black lace bra that she wore underneath.

"Mmm. Sexy," he said. Leaning in, he cupped her left breast through her shirt.

"Bennie!" she protested, pushing his hand away. "They have cameras all over the place."

"So," he said with a grin.

"So, I have to work here, you know."

"You're the one wearing sexy underwear to work."

"I wear it because it is one of the few good bras I have left."

Bennie fell back in the driver's seat, stung by the comment.

Angie looked at her watch, then at her husband. She sighed, torn between consoling him or getting one of the danishes that her department head had delivered every morning. They went quickly.

"Look, Bennie," she finally said. "I didn't mean that the way it sounded."

"It's fine," he said, offering a smile and a dismissive wave. "I know things have been hard on you lately, paying all the bills and stuff. Things are going to get better. I promise."

Angie sighed. Things *had* been hard. Even though she'd worked at least one double a week for months, there was never enough money. They hadn't gone out in forever. She needed lots of things that went unnoticed, new underwear not being the least of them.

"You go impress the hell out of them today. They're getting a good man, Benjamin Howard, don't let them miss that."

"I won't," he said, forcing a smile. "You'd better go. All the donuts will be gone if you hang out much longer."

"They're danishes," she corrected, "But you're right. I gotta go." She leaned over and kissed his cheek. "Love you, babe."

Bennie watched her collect her things and get out of the car. His eyes lingered on her as she walked up to a panel by the door and scanned her badge. She turned and offered two thumbs up, then scurried through the automatic doors before they could close.

While he watched his wife, a reflection on the passenger side window replaced his view of Angie moving through the hospital doors. He glanced over his left shoulder to see if someone had approached the driver's side door. No one was there. Turning back, he found the reflection still there.

He tilted his head, and so did the reflection. Amused, he searched the parking lot again to see what could be causing the reflection. When he looked back, the reflection was more solid, but still transparent. The face staring back at him was vaguely familiar. It could have been him, but not exactly.

He raised his hand, fingers splayed. The reflection in the glass did the same. When he lowered his fingers one by one, the reflection followed suit in perfect unison.

"That's freaky," he said, shaking his head. When the reflection copied him, he noticed hair that was longer and lighter than his. His hair had once been as long as the reflection, but Angie had cut six inches off it a month ago.

His eyes locked on those in the glass. Were his eyes so distant, so empty? He rubbed his eyes with the back of his hand and looked again. The eyes staring back at him were cold and dark, almost solid black against the translucent reflection.

"What the hell?" he asked, beginning to wonder if it was a reflection at all. Bennie leaned over. Resting one hand in the passenger seat, he extended the other toward the window. On the glass, the shape remained still, dark eyes staring intently back at him.

Closer now, he could tell that something wasn't right. The reflection wasn't just on the surface of the glass. It was within the glass itself, the flat edges of the image clearly visible. Also, the image wasn't him, but someone or something trying to look like him.

"What the heck's going on h—"

The beep of a horn stopped Bennie's fingertips just short of the glass. He looked in the rearview mirror at the car behind him. The image in the glass turned in the opposite direction, looking through the back window.

Bennie threw up an apologetic hand before putting the car in gear. Sparing a glance at the window as he pulled away, he thought he saw a smile on the face before it disappeared.

———

Bennie groaned as he came to a stop, barely clearing the cross-traffic lanes. He'd seen the large, orange signs warning of utility work, but in a moment of indecision had run right into it. He could have turned at the last light and found an alternate route, but didn't. The traffic jam in front of him was his punishment for being distracted.

His mind kept telling him that what he saw in the window was simply a reflection, an optical illusion. He didn't believe it. There was something off about it, something dark, like it didn't belong in this world. Not in the light of day anyway.

He sighed and scratched the back of his head. What should have been a nice, easy commute was quickly turning into a headache. After dropping Angie off at the hospital, he'd been marred in traffic at every turn, a concept that was foreign to him. Were there really this many people in town? Did this many people actually go to work at the same time every day? What did they all do?

Resigning himself to wait, Bennie settled into his seat. If he wasn't stuck for long, he'd still make it on time. According to the blue line on the navigation app, the congestion cleared after this intersection, and it was clear sailing the rest of the way. He had about twenty minutes before he had to start worrying.

Looking around, he found himself next to a green four-door car. The driver, an older man with silver hair, had a finger deep up his right nostril. Bennie grimaced and looked away. "Damn man," he moaned.

Movement ahead allowed the nose picker to roll up. His

car was replaced by a white Yukon. When he looked around, the blond passenger was looking back at him. She smiled and shot him a wink. Bennie offered back a wave and a smile of his own.

He'd seen them earlier, before the traffic came to a complete stop. The driver was a large man wearing a tank top. He looked like one of those guys who went to the gym a lot. Of course, none of that mattered. Bennie didn't have any interest in the woman, though she wasn't unattractive.

Ahead of him, someone merged, and his lane moved up one car length. He drew even with the green car, but didn't look at the driver. His new view afforded him a partial view of the utility work that had caused the mess that currently had him trapped. Several men were moving about near the middle of the block, walking back and forth between his lane and the sidewalk. A black man with a clipboard flipped a few pages and then stared at the paper intently. A few seconds later, he looked up and shouted something to the others.

One of the workers, a scrawny kid with the beginning of a beard on his chin, walked up to one of the orange signs, and Bennie's hopes rose. When he pulled out a large black plastic bag and wrapped the sign in it, he knew the end was in sight.

Bennie looked at his phone again. He'd make it with plenty of time to spare. Good. Though he didn't want the job, he'd take it if offered. They needed the money.

The white Yukon moved up beside him, and he garnered another look from the woman passenger. This time, he smiled but didn't wave back. When she raised a hand to smooth her hair, the sun glittered off the ring on her hand. Judging from the size of the diamond, whatever her husband did, he did it well.

The car in front of Bennie moved up, and he followed suit. From here, he could see the crew and the piece of machinery they were using. The contraption had wires hanging out of one end. Bennie traced them across the sidewalk to three different spools hanging from another piece of machinery.

In the lane ahead of him, men were gathering around the machine blocking his path. After a moment of discussion, they began wrangling it toward the edge of the road. One man, thin with long blonde hair, stepped onto the curb and grabbed one end of the machine. He counted to three, and everyone heaved the equipment over the curb.

Bennie sighed. Surely, they'd be free soon, and he could get to his interview. He didn't want to see the disappointment in Angie's eyes if he didn't get the job. He'd seen enough disappointment in her lately to last a lifetime.

The cars in front of Bennie rolled forward slowly, and he followed. As he neared the machine with the cables, the man with long hair turned and looked at him. He held a grimy hard hat in one hand and a cigarette in the other. As Bennie drew even with the guy, he poked the cigarette into the corner of his mouth.

Holding the butt between his thumb and the tip of his pointer finger, he inhaled deeply. He withdrew the cigarette from his mouth, and his eyes locked on Bennie's. His lips puckered. A plume of smoke shot directly at Bennie, covering the distance between them quickly. The worker was ten feet away, but the smoke traveled to Bennie's car, billowing against the glass.

Surprised, Bennie stared at the man, seeing him through the slowly dissipating cloud of smoke. He looked around to see if anyone else noticed it, but everyone was intent on making the light ahead of them.

When he turned back to the worker, he drew in a sharp breath. The distance and angle of the man put his face in the exact spot as the reflection he'd seen earlier. Seen through the smoky haze, the man's features were distorted, giving his face an angular, devilish look.

"What the hell?" Bennie asked, turning to watch him as he rolled past. The man let out a silent laugh, then thumped the cigarette butt at his car.

"Asshole," Bennie complained, throwing up a hand as he

moved toward the traffic light. The two cars ahead of him made it, one just skirting beneath the yellow. Bennie didn't. He grunted in frustration. He wanted to make the light worse than he cared to admit.

When he checked the side mirror for the man, he found him standing on the sidewalk still holding his hard hat beneath one arm. His eyes were narrowed as he stared back at Bennie, but the distant, cold look in them was easy to see. It was something akin to the fabled "thousand-yard stare" among war vets, but more intense, and there was no doubt that it was directed at him.

Bennie looked at the light, drumming his fingers nervously on the steering wheel. "C'mon," he whispered, sparing a glance back at the man. He was still there and still staring. The workers around him moved at a hurried, almost unnatural pace, but he remained perfectly still.

A check on the light told Bennie that it was still red, much to his chagrin. Four lanes of traffic moved from left to right in a constant wave. He rubbed his face with one hand while the other gripped the wheel. His left foot began to bounce nervously as he willed the light to change. "C'mon. Damn you."

Behind him, the man continued to stare, never taking his eyes off Bennie. Then he started toward the car. Bennie's heart began to race, his drumming becoming a light pounding on the steering wheel. "Please," Bennie begged, his nerves unraveling as he stared at the red light.

He checked the man's slow approach in the side mirror. The guy was still ten feet behind him. Bennie's eyes darted to the light, still red, then to the oncoming traffic to his left. If he could catch a break in the traffic, he could turn right and at least be rid of the weird man approaching his car.

Bennie inched as far forward as he dared, his eyes darting between the man and the traffic light. With each step the man took, Bennie's heart pounded harder. Who was he and what did he want? He didn't know the guy, and there was something about him that said he didn't want to.

Finally, the light turned green, and Bennie stomped the gas pedal. Angie's Camry surged forward into the intersection. Bennie was still looking in his side mirror at the man behind him when the black Mercedes slammed into his door.

# CHAPTER FIVE

Carver stared at the watch crystal laying across his fingers, the jointed metal band hanging limply from either side. If he tilted it just so, he could see a vague reflection of himself in the glow of the bathroom light. It wasn't much, just a faint silhouette. No features. Just a shape.

His mind was unsettled this morning. He'd been awake for two hours, and there was no hope of sleep. Much of that time had been spent sitting in the dark listening to the gentle breathing of the woman next to him. Belinda Marcum wasn't a bad companion, as far as companions went.

She had an apartment of her own, a job, and her own car. Though her means were well beneath his, she didn't need him. Carver spared a glance over his shoulder. She was lying on her left side, facing away from him. His eyes traced the curves of her body beneath the covers, and he smiled.

*You should have treated her better.*

Carver recoiled slightly, struck by the voice inside his head. Should have? Past tense? What the hell was that supposed to mean?

Laying the watch aside, he stood. He yawned through a stretch, scratched his ass, and headed for the shower. Since he was up, he might as well get an early start.

————

Downstairs, showered and dressed in his charcoal slacks and crisp white dress shirt, his tie clipped neatly out of the drop zone, Carver leaned over the sink and took a bite of his fried egg on toast sandwich.

As he stood over the sink, chewing slowly, his eyes stared over the counter at the adjacent room. Shadows lurked everywhere, slipping from the corners like ominous fingers. He sipped his coffee, his eyes watching over the mug, for what he did not know.

The voice of his mother crept into his head. "I tell you one thing, sweetheart. This'un is gonna be bad. I can feel it."

In the memory that accompanied his mother's words, they were standing in the backyard of the house he'd grown up in. She was in a simple cotton dress, an ever-present apron about her waist. After taking the last of the clothes off the line, she put her hands on her hips and stared at the darkening western sky.

As if to emphasize her point, miles away, somewhere over Mississippi, a finger of lightning ripped its way across the face of the gathering clouds.

"Might be a night to sleep in the root cellar." She shook her head and picked up the laundry basket, full of the morning's washing.

A sad smile crept across Carver's lips. His mother was a superstitious woman who leaned heavily on omens and signs, gut feelings. "Trust your gut, baby. Remember that. Always trust your gut."

Carver sighed and took another bite of the sandwich. Ovarian cancer took her ten years ago after a lengthy battle. Sheer willpower and stubbornness had held it at bay until she couldn't fight it anymore. She was the strongest person he'd ever known, but in the end, she wasn't strong enough.

At the end, she slept a lot. One night, slumped in a chair at her bedside, he woke with a jolt. Looking around, he found her staring at him. Tear stains marked her cheeks. He asked if she was okay, if she needed more pain meds. They talked for a while, and she said, "I'm so proud of you, baby. Your father is, too. Promise me something. Don't spend so much time chasing the things you want that you miss out on the things you need." He made the promise, and she drifted off to sleep again.

His brow creased as he tried to remember the last time

he'd thought about her outside of a passing memory. It had been months. Probably on her birthday. So why now? Why this morning?

Carver laid the sandwich aside, his appetite suddenly waning. He'd have an early lunch if his stomach felt better. Turning with his coffee cup, he leaned against the counter and took another sip.

The kitchen was bright and roomy, modern, and sleek. It was almost a perfect match to the page he'd torn out of a magazine and handed to his interior designer.

There were no long shadows beneath the fluorescent light, still, he felt as if something wasn't right. Nothing major, just slightly off. Like a picture hanging askew or the slightly crooked tile on the master bathroom floor.

*Trust your gut, Carver.* His mother's words echoed through his mind again.

Carver rolled his eyes and took another sip of coffee. The only thing his gut was telling him was that he'd drank too much, then vigorously jostled it around, making love to Belinda last night. He didn't get enough sleep. He wasn't a spring chicken anymore.

He looked at his watch, surprised at how much time had passed. He gulped more coffee, deposited the cup in the sink, and headed upstairs. Belinda was a slow riser, and he'd have to stay on her to get her out of the house on time.

"Belinda," he called, entering the bedroom. The light from the open bathroom door showed him the shape of her body beneath the covers. He rounded the bed with a huff. "C'mon. Time to rise and shine."

When no sound came from the lump of covers, he went to the bed and snatched them back. "Time to get—" His words froze in his throat. It wasn't Belinda under the covers but a man!

The guy lifted his head from the pillow and smiled at Carver. His face was angular, with well-defined lines and a prominent chin. The dark hair on his head was neatly combed. His face was clean-shaven. He wore a dark suit and a red shirt.

Carver staggered backward. The backs of his legs struck a chair, and he fell into it with a grunt, his eyes never leaving the stranger in his bed.

The man rose onto an elbow but made no further attempts to get out of bed. His smile grew as the panic in Carver's eyes worsened.

"Who the hell are you?" Carver demanded, his voice not as strong as he'd wanted.

The man didn't answer but continued smiling.

To his left, Carver heard a toilet flush, then Belinda's voice asking if he was okay. He turned his head slowly, his heart racing in his chest. She stood in the bathroom doorway, dressed in a t-shirt that was too big for her. Light rushed at him from all around her. He stammered her name, saw the confusion on her face.

Turning back to the bed, he gasped. The covers were thrown back haphazardly. Nothing but a sheet and pillow lay on the bed where the man had been.

"Did you trip or something?" Belinda's voice came from a thousand miles away as she came to his side. "Carver? Hun?"

He watched her lean over him. Oh my god, he thought. Am I having a stroke? Carver shook his head, then turned back to the bed. One hand rose unsteadily, pointing to where the man had been.

Belinda looked at the bed, then back to him. "Oh god, don't tell me there was a spider. Was it a spider? A rat? Oh my god. Tell me it wasn't a rat."

Carver shook his head again as he collected himself. "No." His voice sounded weak but not slurred. He didn't have a stroke. "Uh, no. It was-uh— I don't know." He slid a hand over his hair and rubbed the back of his neck as he righted himself in the chair.

"You don't look so good, hun. Are you feeling okay?"

Carver lied with a nod. "I just tripped, is all."

"Well, you look like you've seen a ghost."

Carver forced a chuckle. "No," he said, unsure what he'd seen. "I was just coming to wake you."

Belinda visibly relaxed. "I had to pee. Stupid bladder." She started back to the bed, but Carver caught her wrist. His eyes went to the bed where the man had been.

"Don't go back to bed. You'll never get up on time, and I'll be late. Again."

"Oh, honey," Belinda whined, turning to him. Her hands wrapped around his neck as she moved closer, burying his face in her ample breasts. "Don't you want to join me?"

Carver pulled back. "I'm not saying I don't want to, but I can't. You know I have to go to the office."

She grunted her displeasure. "You wouldn't regret it."

"I'm sure I wouldn't, but my clients might. Instead of enjoying your lovely body like I'd be doing, they'd be sitting in uncomfortable chairs worrying whether or not I would take their case."

"So," she said, pouting. "Let them wait."

Carver sighed with a smile. He took her hands in his. "You know I can't."

"Can't I at least stay a while longer? I don't have to work today. After all, you did keep me up late last night."

Standing, Carver looked at her with a grin. "By my estimates, you were giving as good as you were getting."

"Please."

Carver spared a glance at the bed and shook his head. He had never let Belinda stay, but today he had a different reason to deny her request. He wasn't sure what he saw, but he didn't want her alone in the house with it.

"Not today, babe. Sorry." He slapped her on the butt and walked away. "Since you're not going to work, you won't need a shower."

———

Carver Willis breathed a sigh of relief when he crossed the bridge spanning the Black Warrior River and started down the long, sweeping curve into town. Despite being awake for hours, he'd still ended up behind schedule.

The commute had been merciless. Just out of his driveway, a delivery truck was having difficulties backing into his neighbor's narrow driveway. The truck and the carpenters who'd be using the stacks of wood scattered on the lawn had effectively delayed him ten minutes.

At the stop sign on Eleven, he'd been mired behind seven cars, including "The Old Man" and his insipid pick-up truck. When he finally did make it out, the oncoming traffic all but precluded him from passing.

The black Mercedes floated down the hill and just skirted a yellow light. Making the light didn't help Carver's mood. He'd been cursing the other drivers, and his blood was up. On top of that, the knot in his stomach had tightened to the point that he was wondering if it was just his age, too many drinks, and a late night, or if something might be seriously wrong with him.

And whatever the hell it was that he saw in the bed was the kicker. It was as real as the nose on his face, but then it simply vanished. No person could have gotten into the house and made it upstairs without one of them seeing him. Then they'd have to get into bed during the short time that Belinda used the bathroom. It couldn't have been a man.

Not a regular man.

*Then what was it?*

The brake lights of the car ahead of him snatched Carver from his thoughts. His eyes darted to the rearview mirror. He couldn't pass. His foot found the brake and pushed hard. The Mercedes nosed to a stop just inches from the ancient Chevy Impala in front of him.

Carver let out a long, frustrated groan and slammed his

hand on the steering wheel. The driver of the Impala, an older black man, was staring back at him in his own mirror. Carver met his eyes and threw his hands up, muttering, "Why are you looking at me? You're the dumbass who stopped on a yellow."

Shaking his head to clear it, Carver took in a long, deep breath and let it out slowly. He wasn't far from the office. He needed to get his head on straight. His secretary would be in soon after him, and he didn't want her to see him all flustered. There'd be questions. Questions he didn't have the answers to.

Besides, he couldn't risk rear-ending someone. As soon as they found out he was a lawyer, they'd probably develop neck pain or anxiety or some other shit. He knew all the tricks because he used them regularly. To date, not many other lawyers have found a way around them, and he doubted if he could either. In the words of his mentor, "Pain is hard to disprove."

When the light finally turned green, the pack of cars began to move. They made it one block before Carver was shouting again. He hated traffic, sure that the only reason it existed was because of stupid people. Either stupid city planners, stupid drivers, or someone else stupid.

The cars moved forward as one tight group. Carver looked around for an opening, but there was none. His shoulders tensed. His grip tightened on the steering wheel. The knot in his stomach got worse. He clenched his teeth while his eyes searched for an opening.

The engine of the Mercedes purred beneath him like a greyhound begging to be set loose. If he could just get a little bit of an opening. "Stupid traffic," he grumbled.

Rolling along with the other commuters, his eyes wandered to the buildings lining the left side of the road. He was approaching a three-story brick monstrosity painted dark green and trimmed in white. His mind tried to recall what it had been. Maybe the old phone company? Back when everyone had landlines. He couldn't remember.

His eyes washed down the building to the wide concrete steps that led to the main entrance of the building, now boarded up. At the top of the steps, a man was leaning against the wall of the recessed entry. The gray jacket of his suit was thrown over his shoulder, held by one of the man's long fingers.

As Carver approached, the man turned and looked directly at him. The part in his hair was clean and perfectly straight, his pale scalp clearly visible. His long, angular face defined his prominent features. His cleanly shaven cheeks were slightly sunken.

As Carver drew even, the man raised a cigarette trapped between two of the fingers on his left hand and took a long drag from it. With his eyes still locked on Carver, he blew a long plume of smoke right at him.

Carver's heart stopped in his chest when he recognized the man. It was the same man from his bed this morning! He was sure of it. It had to be him. Carver's head turned as he rolled past, watching the man watch him. When the guy smiled, he was sure. He'd never forget that smile. It looked like someone was cutting him open, but he was trying desperately not to show that it hurt.

Ahead of Carver, the Impala slowed. The brake lights pulled his attention back to the road. Ahead, the light was turning yellow. If he didn't do something, he'd be trapped here with this strange man staring at him until the light changed. Suddenly, he wanted to be anywhere else.

He looked around the Impala and found the lane next to them clear. His eyes darted to the mirror as he started to ease over. A black SUV was coming up fast, but he had time. He maneuvered the Mercedes around the Impala and pressed the gas.

Ahead of them, a small green smart car skirted beneath the next light. In an instant, Carver's eyes darted to the cross traffic lined against the intersecting light, then back to the signal in front of him. His foot sank on the accelerator.

A flash of color snatched his eyes down from the signal, now glowing red. The side of a silver car filled his view, and everything else in the world disappeared. The driver, a young man with collar-length sandy brown hair, was looking back at something on the sidewalk. He didn't even check for cross traffic. He was in a hurry to get somewhere. He never saw the Mercedes coming.

Carver's foot moved to the brake, but it was too late. His final thought wasn't of his money or his practice but of Belinda. Then the world went black.

# CHAPTER SIX

Bennie pulled the chain on the porcelain fixture over the bathroom sink. The bulb that wasn't burned out cast a pale light over the small room like it was already tired of fighting the darkness. The rental that he and his wife had called home for nearly ten years was in dire need of renovation, but since their rent was always late, they didn't have a leg to stand on when it came to complaints.

He looked at himself in the mirror with a moan. He didn't feel good. Not bad, just not good. It was like the second day after a really bad drunk. Like that time in Roanoke. He had a long-distance fight with Angie. It was four days before Christmas. She wanted him home, but they'd been asked to stay over for another show. She ended up hanging up on him, and he tried to drink every ounce of whiskey left in the city. He'd awakened late the next day in the bathtub of the cheap motel they were staying in. There was dried puke on his shirt, and he'd pissed himself.

He called Angie, apologized, and begged her forgiveness. She was short with him but finally gave in. They did the show, not one of their best, and he'd gone directly back to bed. He woke up the next morning at check-out feeling better, but still not well.

That was exactly how he felt now.

Bennie put a hand on either side of the sink and leaned in, staring at his own reflection. The lines on his face told him some hard truths he didn't want to hear. He was closer to forty than thirty. His band was gone, and he didn't have any prospects. His life was in shambles. His dream was dead as a doornail.

Nobody had called like he thought they would. He was living off odd jobs and the eternal patience of his wife. Though she didn't mention it, he knew the bills were overdue. She'd always been so supportive, but her back was against the wall.

Their backs were against the wall.

Through the years, he'd always kept odd jobs as long as they didn't interfere with his playing guitar. They didn't pay well, but it was money. Coupled with Angie's pay as an X-ray tech and the money he made gigging, they'd done okay.

He'd bused tables, laid sod, and even worked the drive-thru at Burger Heaven. His friends gave him shit for that one, but he didn't mind. They paid eleven bucks an hour, and the work was easy.

"All we need is one big break," he'd told her. "The right guy walks in on the right night, and we'll be set, baby. Set for life." She might not have believed him, but he believed himself. He'd told himself that line more than he'd told it to Angie. Along with a lot of other ones.

*Breaking into the music business is hard. Sometimes you have to be luckier than good. It's not about talent, it's about who you know. It will happen one day.*

After the band broke up, things began to change. He'd spent an easy month sleeping in, strumming his guitar, and jotting down song lyrics. As time passed, Angie's patience began to wane. Just little comments asking if anyone had called looking for a guitarist. That slowly morphed into hints at job openings, you know, just until someone calls.

When she'd come out and said that she thought he needed something constructive to do, he'd gone out and found a job. Stung by her comment, he took the first thing the woman behind the desk at the employment center offered him.

The next day, Angie dropped him off at dawn in the middle of nowhere. He spent the next fifteen hours stabbing the pointed end of an eight-pound metal bar into the rocky soil of a surface mine. Into each hole created by the bar, he'd drop one scrawny pine sapling, then push the dirt up to it with his foot.

He got paid per tree, and no matter how hard he tried, he couldn't keep up with the others. All day, he listened to them speaking in Spanish, laughing occasionally when they looked at him, and the sound of the bar stabbing into the hard ground.

He came home with a screaming back, blisters on both hands, and wreaking of pine, raw metal, and sweat. He showered and collapsed onto the couch, managing to choke down a plate of Hamburger Helper before falling asleep. Four days later, he handed Angie a check for three hundred twelve dollars and eighteen cents, after taxes.

She told him not to go back. He didn't argue.

————

Bennie sighed and shook his head. This time, things felt different. Not only was there a sense of urgency, but also one of permanence. They weren't just between gigs. Not this time.

He'd filled out an application with a local construction company. Angie told him that her father said it was a big outfit. Lots of potential for growth. He could move on up the ladder with hard work and dedication. Of course, the fact that he didn't know shit from shinola when it came to construction didn't seem to factor into his father-in-law's train of thought.

The bum that his baby girl had married was finally getting a "real job". That was all he needed to know. Of course, there weren't any openings in the office building where he worked. Not even in the mail room. All that stuff is subbed out, you see. Nothing he could do.

Bennie closed his eyes and sighed, wondering if all those years with the band were just a waste of time. It hurt to think that they might have been, so he pushed the thought from his head. Almost.

————

Bennie pulled out a chair and sat at the kitchen table with his cup of coffee. Its joints loosened by use, the chair wobbled slightly, then settled in beneath his weight. He made a mental note to swap the chairs he and Angie used when they didn't eat in front of the television with the others in the set. The unused two, one trapped against the wall by the table and the other supporting a stack of old magazines, still looked new.

Sitting without a shirt, his only company was the steam from his coffee and the silence of the house around him. And, of course, his thoughts.

Angie just didn't know how it felt to be him, to have this feeling inside and the need to let it out. She'd never written a song, played it for strangers. It was exhilarating to have a song come together, the chorus, the bridge, the music, and feel it in your bones. Then you play it for others, waiting breathlessly for one, maybe two seconds as the music dies to discover their reaction. When the thunder of applause finally came, the relief.

Angie had once called him an "adrenaline junkie," but it was so much more than that. His soul ached to play music, his music. On days he worked his day jobs and was too tired to play, it felt like he lost a part of himself. The only thing that kept him going was knowing that he could play tomorrow.

There was always tomorrow.

After a string of "tomorrows" that never came, depression began to set in. After a week, he didn't even want to play anymore. All he wanted to do was sleep and mourn whatever was within him that was dying.

He explained to Angie how it felt early in their relationship, when they were younger, and their love was new. He talked about how it was a part of him, not just what he did. How it was a need, not a want. She'd thought that it was so fascinating. So interesting. Now, those days were so far gone that he wondered if they'd ever happened at all.

He'd met the bright-eyed, naïve version of Angie at a show in Mobile. She and some of her girlfriends had driven over from Gulf Shores to see the band. She wore a short, black leather miniskirt and a skin-tight tank top. Back then, she had multiple ear piercings and wore a sort of quasi-goth makeup, especially on her eyes.

She was nervous when they brought her and her friends backstage. Her friends fell instantly into the arms of two of his bandmates. Within minutes, they were doing some heavy making out. He could tell that Angie liked him, but was shy. Her smile was genuine, sincere. She was just what he'd been looking for.

They spent most of the night walking on the waterfront and ended up on a beach. They did kiss some, but that was as far as it went. She wasn't like the other girls who worked their way through the crowd to the front row. She wasn't a party girl. That's what he liked about her.

———

When two arms slipped around him from behind, Bennie jumped. His hand struck the cup, sending coffee pouring across the table.

"I'm sorry," Angie said, running for a dishcloth. "I didn't mean to scare you."

"Damn, Ange. Slipping up behind me like that."

"I'm sorry," she said with a chuckle as she returned with a dishcloth and began swabbing up the coffee.

Bennie conceded a grin of his own as he watched her take the soaked rag to the sink, one hand beneath it to catch any drips.

"Were you asleep?" she asked, returning with a dry towel.

"No, just thinking."

She laid the cloth over the remaining coffee and grabbed his cup. "Let me refill that for you." She went to the coffee pot and filled his cup, then poured one for herself. "What were you thinking about so hard?" she asked, joining him at the table.

"The night we met, after that show in Mobile."

Angie rolled her eyes with a huff. "I was too afraid to go goth, so I ended up looking like some crazy person who couldn't make up her mind."

"You ended up looking beautiful," he told her, his hand finding hers.

"That eye makeup." She shook her head. "It's a wonder

you'd even look at me without laughing."

"I did." A reminiscent smile spread across his face. "Things were so different back then, weren't they?"

"We were different. I was in tech school. My dad was paying my bills and giving me an allowance, and you were touring around, crashing in cheap flea-bag motels, or sleeping in that hooptie van y'all had."

When their shared laughter died, Bennie looked at her. "You ever miss those days?"

Angie shrugged with a sigh. "Maybe every now and then, you know. Not having to worry about adult stuff, no bills, or taxes. No boss." She sipped her coffee. "I miss being a size four."

Bennie nodded. She'd changed a lot, but not in a bad way. She'd always been more responsible with money than him. She liked things more orderly, more defined, but was still carefree enough to enjoy his chaotic lifestyle. On Fridays, after her classes, she'd drive to Birmingham or Atlanta to hang out with them. Once, after they'd started getting a following, she'd skipped some of her classes altogether and had traveled with them to do shows in Dallas and Galveston, Texas.

When things started getting serious between them, he did his best to steer the band to shows closer to home, even balking at a far west coast swing just to be with her. Now, he often wondered what might have been if they'd gone to California. They might have played in some big clubs and maybe even met the right people. They might be household names by now. Money wouldn't be an issue, and he wouldn't be getting ready to take a construction job.

"What happened to those carefree kids?" Bennie asked.

"We grew up," Angie said flatly.

"Did we grow up, or did we just give up?"

"What's that supposed to mean?" she asked, her coffee cup halfway to her lips.

"I don't know. Nothing, I guess."

Angie sipped her coffee and set the cup down. "Well, either way, we have bills to pay, Bennie. We gotta eat, gotta have lights that come on. Rent. Heat. You know. All that takes money."

"I know it does, Ange. Damn. I'm not a kid, you know."

"That's my point. We're *not* kids anymore." She pushed up from the table and grabbed her cup. "I have to get ready for work." She walked away, leaving Bennie with a feeling that he couldn't explain. It was a mixture of sadness, anger, and indignation.

"Welcome to Grownup Ville," he said to the empty room. "Where dreams go to die."

———

Between the cars on the next block, Bennie glimpsed a tiny sliver of bright orange and groaned. It was the color reserved for one thing and one thing only: road work.

The slow creep of bumper-to-bumper traffic had allowed his thoughts to wander. His mind began conjuring what his life would be like if he accepted life in suburbia.

On Friday nights, they'd have friends over. Maybe one of Angie's co-workers. Of course, she'd bring her husband. Maybe some muscle-bound jerk named Derrick. No, Bruce.

Bruce would be a plumber and would make playful digs at construction workers. He'd offer to try and get Bennie a job with his company, to 'Make an honest man out of you'. The girls would talk about their boss over pot roast while he sat in silent misery, dying inside of a plaid short-sleeved dress shirt.

After supper, he'd take Bruce out back to have a beer or two. Maybe show him the new grill. Bruce would volunteer tips on his lawn, ask how his and Angie's love life was.

He'd try to deflect, to avoid the question with a shrug. Maybe he'd say it was okay even though it wasn't. Bruce would wonder if his old lady was giving it to someone else and complain that he never got any. Of course, the fact that she still had a nice rack made it worse. Ole Bruce was a boob man and couldn't keep his hands off 'em.

A polite beep drug Bennie out of his thoughts. The light was green, and there was just enough room for two cars to squeeze in on the next block. He drove beneath the light, coming to rest behind a red Ford Taurus. The road signs were easier to see now. 'Utility Work' glared back at him from a diamond-shaped field of safety orange.

Bennie groaned, trying to clear his head. Inside his chest, his heart was racing. Could he do it? Could he actually give up his music for that? To him, it didn't sound like a fair deal. Trading everything he ever wanted for a mortgage and stress over the economy sounded like torture. It sounded like hell.

He rolled up a car length as the Taurus merged into the lane beside him, freeing up space. There were now only two cars between him and the utility crew. Yellow hard hats bobbed around above the cars in front of him, moved by unseen heads. There was a mechanical, grinding noise. The hard hats were all around the source.

The noise ended suddenly. Bennie watched the hard hats converge in one place with rapt attention. Would he have to wear a hard hat if he got the job he was applying for?

A hand came up, waving, then disappeared. Men came from the sidewalk and mixed with the group of workers in the street. One hard hat, a white one, moved to the sidewalk. The man beneath it turned in his direction and said something. A younger man in a bright yellow mesh vest started toward the orange sign with a large black bag. Bennie watched him cover the sign, then retreat. That'll be me, he thought, one side of his mouth pulling into a frown. Low man on the totem pole. Shit rolls downhill.

The hard hats divided into two groups facing each other. The ones on the left dipped then rose again. The ones on the right backed their way onto the sidewalk. Leaning over into the passenger seat, Bennie caught sight of a wheeled machine roughly half the size of Angie's car. Long cables protruded from one end and lay on the sidewalk. His brow furrowed, his head tilting to one side.

The sight of the black cables on the sidewalk seemed familiar somehow, like he'd seen this scene before. He didn't have any specific memory of it, just a feeling. Of course, it was possible. It was getting into spring. As the weather warmed, everyone in town would enter into "road work season". It was the inescapable price of progress.

When the car in front of him moved, Bennie matched its progress, and more of the workers came into view. Most of them were either tending to the machine or the cables coming out of it. All but one. A tall, gaunt-looking man was standing a few feet from the others, his hard hat held against the side of his yellow safety vest by one limp arm.

Bennie's eyes met his as the Camry rolled forward and stopped. The man's eyes were dark and sunken. His face was angular and pale. A thin wisp of smoke rose from the cigarette hanging from the corner of his mouth.

Bennie recoiled slightly, finding something unsettling in the man's stare. Still, he was unable to look away. The man's free hand came up and pinched the cigarette angrily, moving it to the center of his lips. The ember glowed for a long time, then faded. The man plucked the cigarette from his lips and puckered. A long plume of smoke escaped his wrinkled lips and flew right at Bennie.

Though still a distance away, the smoke shot straight at him like a gray finger before crashing against the passenger side window. The smoke billowed against the glass like ocean waves, rolling outward. Through the dissipating smoke, Bennie saw a grin come to the man's lips as he rolled slowly past. The smoke lent the man's face a devilish look, making the grin more ominous.

Becoming aware that he was still moving, Bennie snatched his head around. The light in front of them was green. He spared a glance over his shoulder at the man just in time to catch the sight of his cigarette tumbling through the air. It hit the window, throwing tiny red sparks into the air before bouncing off and falling away.

"What the hell?" Bennie asked. He looked around just as the car ahead of him skirted beneath the traffic light, now turning red. He cursed his luck and rolled to a stop.

In the side mirror, he found the man again. He was still staring, his coworkers moving around him as if he wasn't there. Bennie's eyes narrowed, watching the grin fade from the stranger's face. The grin was bad, but without it, the face took on a sullen, angry look.

Bennie's eyes darted between the traffic light and the side mirror. The light was still red. The man was still staring. The light was still red. Bennie gasped quietly when he looked back at the worker. He was still staring, but was he closer now?

"C'mon, man," Bennie pleaded to the traffic signal. Back in the mirror, the man was closer still, less than five feet from the back of the car.

"Shit," Bennie whispered through his teeth. The light was still red. The stranger was now even with his trunk. Bennie inched forward, closer to the crossing traffic.

"What is this dude's problem?"

In the mirror, the man was close enough for Bennie to see through the mesh vest. The plain white t-shirt he wore was wrinkled badly, like he'd slept in it. There was a light scruff on the man's square chin. His eyes were dark shadows. The workers moving around behind him were a blur, their world out of focus.

Bennie's pulse quickened as the stranger drew even with his car again. He'd be able to see him over his shoulder if he dared to turn. His eyes went back to the traffic signal. Still red, but cross traffic had stopped. He offered one more glance at the stranger. When he looked back at the light, it was turning green.

Bennie stomped the gas pedal, springing across the

crosswalk painted on the road and into the path of an oncoming car. His eyes were still watching the stranger when the black Mercedes slammed into his door.

# CHAPTER SEVEN

Carver lay in his bed, one arm tucked behind his head, craving a cigarette. It had been so long since he'd wanted one that it almost felt foreign. Almost.

He laid them down cold turkey almost seventeen years ago. His father worked his whole life only to end up with COPD, and he was determined not to go out like that. In the weeks and months after he quit, cravings would pop up at odd moments. Once, he'd been in a meeting with the opposing counsel, and the urge struck. There was a hint of smoke on the guy's suit coat, and it hit him like a ton of bricks. He'd been so distracted that he almost cost his client and himself a lot of money.

That was the last strong craving he had. For years, they'd come, softly, almost as an afterthought. After a good meal, sometimes after sex.

He sighed and decided that it must have been ten years or more since he'd wanted a cigarette. Longer since he'd craved one so badly. He'd had a good meal at Antonelli's, a small dish of ravioli, a salad, and bread with a nice dry red wine. He hadn't wanted a cigarette then. He'd also had a nice bout of sex with Belinda and hadn't wanted one afterward.

So, what was it? Why now?

He knew the answer before he asked it. He was troubled. No, not exactly troubled. Unsettled was a better word. He'd awakened in the night, and although he needed to relieve himself, it wasn't urgent enough to awaken him.

It was a dream that woke him, but he couldn't remember it now. Only that it wasn't pleasant. Lying in the darkness, accompanied only by Belinda's gentle breathing, he tried to remember what it was that had his heart beating fast and his palms sweaty.

He drew in a deep breath and let it out slowly as another craving struck, determining that he wasn't going to start smoking again. He wouldn't go back to huddling on stoops in the cold and the rain. There'd be no more skulking away as old women approached, giving him the side eye as they clutched their tiny purses to their chest as if it were a shield against second-hand smoke.

Carver Willis sat up on the edge of the bed in his boxer shorts. He knew he didn't have to worry about waking Belinda. She was a heavy sleeper, but a part of him wished she wasn't. He looked back at the curve of her hip beneath the covers, and a smile almost came to his lips.

They'd been more or less steady for a while now, and if forced, he'd concede that his feelings for her were more than physical. She wasn't the brightest bulb sometimes, but she was pleasant enough company. She never asked him for much more than his time and didn't lean on him to get married.

He stiffened, drawing in a sharp breath as a cold hand landed on his back. His mind told him that the hand was gray and ashy, that it had black nails at the end of elongated fingers. That it belonged to a monster. A scream rose in his throat.

"Are you okay, hun?"

Belinda's voice washed away the spike of fear, and Carver relaxed. He rubbed away the tiny beads of sweat that sprang up on his brow and cleared his throat.

"Yeah, I'm okay," he lied, still shaken by the trick his mind had played on him.

A warm body pressed against his back, and two arms snaked around his waist. Belinda placed a kiss at the base of his neck. "You're up early."

"Yeah," he said, rubbing her arm. "I couldn't sleep."

"Is it your belly?" she asked, her head laid against his back. One hand moved and rubbed his stomach. "Need me to get you a Tums?"

Carver smiled and put his hand over hers. "Nah, babe. It's not my stomach."

A mumbled "Okay" drifted over his shoulder.

Carver sat in the darkness, absorbing Belinda's weight as she fell back asleep in increments. Her grip loosened. Her breasts pressed against him through the thin cotton t-shirt she wore. Her breath was hot on his bare skin.

He sat and thought about the fact that he'd almost panicked when she touched him. Of course, he hadn't expected it, but it was a far greater leap than any rational person would make. The hand of a monster with long gray fingers and black nails was a long way from the slim hand of the woman sleeping next to him.

His brow furrowed as his unease grew. Something was off. Wrong somehow. *Trust your gut, Carver.* His mother's words echoed through his mind, and he was a kid again, standing in his yard while storm clouds gathered to the west. Lightning slashed across the darkening sky. A storm was coming.

———

The razor glided through the shaving cream with a decisive stroke, leaving a clean path across Carver's left cheek. In the mirror, his eyes narrowed defiantly, following the razor's course as it made another pass. The time it took to get Belinda situated back in bed and for him to take a long, hot shower had given him time to think.

Something was off. He didn't know what, but he knew something was wrong. His waking early, the odd feeling in his gut, and then the instant of panic. They were all symptoms of a larger problem. He didn't like problems and set his mind to meeting this one head-on.

In the shower, he mentally reviewed his current cases but found no loose ends that could bite him in the ass. Still, he'd have his team double-check all of them. He went over the short list of people he trusted and the long list of those he didn't, without finding an imminent problem. There were some minor quibbles, but nothing he hadn't known about for months.

Whatever it was, it had to be personal. He examined and reexamined his relationship with Belinda, but there was nothing there that threw up any red flags.

He thought about his younger brother. He was living in Florida, and when they'd talked last, three weeks ago, everything was well. The wife was good, still teaching second grade. Their two boys were fine. The youngest, Forrest, was having some allergy problems, but that was about it.

The only person left who was of any consequence was his father. They talked at least every other week, and despite his age and condition, he was still very sharp in his mind and his tongue. The old fart would probably outlive him by a long shot.

The razor came off his chin and sank into the sink, disappearing beneath clumps of shaving cream floating like icebergs in the cloudy water. He tilted his chin upwards slightly and brought the razor up to shave his neck, but stopped suddenly.

In the mirror, he saw a drop of water, tinged in red, collect on the edge of the razor and drip into the sink. His eyes shifted from the reflection to the razor in his fingers. Another drop of red water slid down the blades and ran over the edge. His eyes followed it to the sink. Blood hit the water and blossomed outward in every direction.

"Dammit," he muttered, putting the razor aside. He grabbed a towel and wiped his face. Tilting his chin from side to side, he examined his face and neck. Fingertips probed and flattened the skin, finding nothing. Carver took a deep breath and let it out slowly. Was this like the image his mind had conjured when Belinda touched him?

He leaned closer to the mirror, staring at his reflection for a long time. The eyes staring back at him were defiant, almost angry, but there was a hint of fear in them that he didn't like.

"Get your shit together, Carver. Now." He stared at himself

a minute longer, then lathered his neck again. He watched it in the mirror for a moment, waiting to see if the blood would make another appearance. When nothing happened, he shook his head and finished shaving.

———

His day had started much earlier and with more bother than usual, so when Carver rode Highway Eleven into Souls Harbor, he was nearly irate. His anger at the traffic had pushed his early morning worries to the side. He'd hoped to get an early start reviewing files, but his fellow commuters seemed to be intent on slowing him.

He stayed on the accelerator as he glided through the long, sweeping curve and started the descent into the town itself. Ahead, the light was green. The lights were timed so if he could make the first one, he'd probably make it to his office without being caught.

As he neared the light, a new color on the right sidewalk caught his attention. A large orange sign sat propped on a stand informing them that utility work was going on somewhere ahead. Carver clenched his jaw. There always seemed to be something with the roads around here.

The black Mercedes just skirted beneath the light as it turned yellow. He smiled, but it was short-lived. Traffic in front of him had slowed. His foot lifted from the accelerator, hovering hopefully above it. The sea of brake lights in front of him forced his foot to shift to the brake, and he slowed quickly, cursing his luck.

His eyes darted from lane to lane, desperately seeking an opening. A dark gray sedan was to his left. A large white SUV followed it closely. To his right, a black SUV—a smaller, sportier type than the white one—occupied the lane beside him.

"Shit," he said, his shoulders slumping as he settled into the seat. "Perfect." The rumble of the car in front of him, an Impala that had to be nearing his age, drowned out the purr of his own engine. Carver's eyes went to the hole in the middle of the trunk lid. The term "rusty asshole" drifted to the front of his mind.

He hadn't been born into such privilege that he didn't know what happened to the trunk of the Impala. Cars of that era had an ignition key and a trunk key. If the trunk key was lost, all you had to do was beat the lock out, then you could open the trunk with a flathead screwdriver. Someone had lost the Impala's trunk key.

When traffic began rolling again, slowly like a herd of cattle, Carver began searching for an opening. To his left, the SUV dominated the space. The young brunette driving it, all one hundred pounds of her, seemed content to go with the flow. There was no hope there.

Ahead of her, the old man in the gray sedan had his hands at ten and two and his eyes fixed on the back of the white van in front of him. Carver growled in frustration.

The façade of a three-story brick building loomed over the van. The paint, once dark green, had faded considerably, but even if it hadn't, it wouldn't have fit the surroundings. There was a For Sale sign in one of the large front windows. It had been there for months. Whoever bought it would have to spend a pretty penny to bring it in line with the rest of downtown.

Carver's eyes fell to his side mirror. The young man in the orange Dodge Charger behind the balding man in the sporty SUV was dawdling. A space of five feet had opened up. Carver's eyes darted to the traffic in front of him. It was moving slowly, but it was moving.

His eyes dropped back to the mirror. The kid was looking at his phone. Carver smiled. A few more inches, and he could move over. Even if he got stuck behind the old man, he'd eventually have to turn anyway.

More space opened up as they rolled through the light. His eyes darted to the white SUV next to him. He was still looking in that direction when the back of the car cleared the front steps of the green building. His eyes locked on a figure standing on top of the concrete steps leading to the sidewalk. He didn't know why, but his mouth suddenly went dry.

From this distance, all he could tell was that it was a white man in a dark suit. His eyes stayed on the man, watching traffic out of his periphery. There was something about him. Did he know him? It was doubtful. Why would anyone he knew be hanging out in front of a vacant building?

The man, who'd been looking down at the cigarette in his hand, lifted his eyes to the traffic in front of him. He watched it for a few seconds, then his head slowly turned toward Carver. When their eyes met, an idea exploded in Carver's mind, and he gasped.

In an instant, Carver scanned the area in front of the building. There was a narrow lane next to a curb that had been painted yellow.

In his mirror, the Charger hadn't made up any ground. His hands and foot worked in unison, giving the car gas and yanking the steering wheel to the left. The black Mercedes slipped into the lane, narrowly missing the Charger, and drawing a quick blast of its horn.

In one fluid motion, Carver passed through the lane and into the fire lane against the yellow curb. He stomped the brakes, and the Mercedes came to a screeching halt twenty feet short of the entrance to the building.

The man looked at him with a mixture of surprise and something that might have been relief. He slipped his suit coat off and hung it over his right shoulder, one finger hooked in the loop beneath the collar to hold it there. He stood like he didn't have a care in the world as he watched Carver approach in long, urgent strides.

"Well, hello, Mister Willis." His voice was calm and deep, soothing. There was no hint of any accent at all. Local or otherwise.

"Who the hell are you?" Carver asked, looking up at the man as he leaned against the wall of the inset doorway.

The man took a draw from his cigarette, enjoyed it for a moment, then blew the smoke over Carver's head. "That is a difficult question to answer."

"How do you know my name?" Carver asked.

The man smiled as if he were talking to a child, as if he had some not-so-good news and didn't quite know how to tell him. "That, too, is complicated."

"Look," Carver pointed a finger at the man as he put a foot on the bottom step. "There's something going on. I don't know what, but it's something."

The man nodded slightly. "Indeed, there is."

Carver threw his hand up and let it drop. "Look, man. I'm a lawyer. I know how to talk around a question, and I know it when I see it."

The man nodded in agreement but simply took another draw from the cigarette pinned between his pointer and index finger.

"So, you want to tell me what the hell is going on?"

A slight chuckle escaped the man's lips. "I'm just enjoying a smoke on this fine spring morning, Mister Willis. You're the one who almost caused an accident swerving across lanes of traffic to get here." He shrugged one shoulder. "And here you are."

Carver's eyes narrowed as he stared at the man. His mind was turning flips as it tried to figure things out. He didn't know this man, so why had he taken such drastic measures to get to him? Why was his gut telling him that this man was important, that he was connected to the feeling he'd had all morning? And what about the blood on his razor? Was he responsible for that, too?

"What are you?" Carver finally asked, though not as demanding.

"That would be as difficult to answer as who I am."

"What's with the riddles and double talk? You got a name, Mister?"

The name chuckled lightly. "I've been called a lot of things, but no, I don't have a name."

"I'm about tired of this crap." Carver moved to mount the first step but stopped so suddenly that he almost fell back. He gathered himself and stared up at the man. "What the hell?" His voice sounded weak, like air escaping a deflating balloon.

Carver stood frozen, watching as the stranger pushed off the wall. He took another draw from the cigarette and thumped it aside casually. The drone of traffic behind him faded to a whisper. The world around him darkened at the edges like one of those old-time photos people got at the mall.

The man moved forward slowly, casually. He took the steps effortlessly, the hard soles of his black wingtips striking each concrete step like a bell toll. His eyes never left Carver.

In his chest, Carver felt his heart rate climb. Sweat collected at his temples. His own breath moved in and out in desperate pants. He wanted to run, but his feet wouldn't move.

"I think it's time to go. You don't want to be late."

"Late for what?" Carver asked dumbly.

The man smiled and lifted a hand.

Carver's eyes darted from the man's dark eyes to the hand now in front of him. The skin was dry and gray, like ashes. Dark grime had collected beneath his ragged nails and in the cuticle beds. Four fingers curled downward, meeting his thumb. Lines appeared in the ash at his knuckles, revealing black, uneven creases.

One long finger moved toward him in slow motion. His eyes fixed on the tip as it came closer. When it tilted slightly upward, he noticed that there was no fingerprint on the pad. The tip of the finger drew closer until it gently touched his forehead between his eyes. For Carver, the world went black, and he was suddenly falling from a great height.

———

A long, angry horn blast snatched Carver out of his trance. Near panic, he looked around frantically. He was back in his car, back in traffic. There was no man with dirty hands.

With his heart still racing and sweat still clinging to his temples, his foot pressed the gas pedal. The Mercedes jumped into the intersection, rolling beneath the green light.

His eyes darted to each of his mirrors. He passed a black SUV rolling slowly through the intersection. Barely checking to see if it was clear, he swerved in front of it, drawing a quick honk of protest.

He never looked back, obeying the one thing his mind had seized on. Go. He had to go. It didn't matter where; he just had to get away from here. He'd never been so sure of anything in his life. Just fucking go.

He skirted beneath the next light with the rest of the cars around him. The antique Impala next to him barely drew a glance. As did the green monster of a building that usually drew his eye. It sailed past him in a blur.

Ahead of him, the light was already yellow, but he never considered stopping. He had to go. He could make it if he hurried. His foot sank on the accelerator. His eyes darted to the mirror, then back to the road. The light turned red, but he didn't stop. He couldn't. Something silver flashed before his eyes. His foot moved to the brake, but never pressed it.

# CHAPTER EIGHT

Bennie sat on the steps of his tiny front porch in a pair of jeans and a faded Pensacola Beach t-shirt. A Fender Stratocaster with a lot of miles on it rested across his lap. His left hand gripped the neck while his right held a coffee cup. The hot coffee helped fend off the predawn chill in the air.

Setting the cup aside, he bent over the guitar and continued strumming gently. He wasn't playing a song, just bits and pieces of anything that came to mind. He'd awakened in the middle of the night with an incessant need to play. When he lifted the guitar from the stand in the bedroom he shared with Angie, his wife, there was dust on it. It was one of the saddest things he'd ever seen, and the need to apologize rose in his chest.

Lying in the dark next to Angie, he'd listened to her steady breathing and made the decision to commit to the job he was interviewing for today. If they hired him, he'd work his ass off this summer and make some money, pay some bills. It'd take a load off Angie and hopefully alleviate the nagging feeling that he was a deadbeat.

It had been nearly a year since his band, Midnight Blue, broke up, and no one had called like he thought they would. He'd even humbled himself to make a few calls, putting the word out that he was looking for a spot. He silently absorbed the pity in the voices of those who used to be his contemporaries, storing it with the rest of his shame.

They had a good run. Almost eleven years. He'd made a living playing music for over a decade, with a few odd jobs thrown in during extended dry spells. They flirted with record deals, but none ever came. In the end, they'd simply flamed out and walked away. He'd failed.

"If the truth means that it's over…" he sang in a whisper, making up lyrics as he strummed the guitar gently. "Then please, baby, tell me lies. 'Cause I'm stuck here in a prison… where dreams go to die. I might be losing my mind… I might be going crazy. Or just waiting for death to come…in a big black Mercedes."

Bennie shook his head with a chuckle. "Damn, man," he said. "That went south quick." He laid the guitar on the floor beside him and picked up his coffee cup. His eyes watched over the rim as a pickup rolled past on the street. The interior lights illuminated a middle-aged man with a full beard and sleepy eyes. Bennie half raised a hand to wave. The man didn't look his way. Tools rattled in the bed of the truck when it hit a pothole in front of their mailbox.

Bennie propped an elbow on his knee and pushed one hand through his hair. He bent and rested his head against his palm, staring at the sidewalk in front of him. A crack in the weathered concrete was full of spring weeds, their shapes vague in the distant light of the coming day.

A wave of emotion welled in his chest. It was one of profound sadness but also regret. It felt like something was ending. Something big.

He took a deep breath and released it slowly, surprised to find that his eyes had welled with tears. He knew what depression felt like, but this wasn't it. The feelings were dark. Ominous.

"Shake it off, man," he told himself as he sat up. He hadn't slept much, waking several times in the night. He was nervous about the job interview he had today. As bad as he didn't want to take a job as a carpenter, he also dreaded having to tell his wife that he didn't get it. His music career had crashed and burned, and this was his penance. He had to do something to make money.

"Maybe by the fall things will change," he said, shaking his head.

"You want some company, or do you want to keep talking

to yourself?"

Bennie jumped at the voice behind him, spilling coffee down his pant leg.

"I'm sorry," Angie said, coming to him from the doorway. "I thought you heard me open the door."

"It's fine." Bennie wiped at his wet jeans. "Come. Sit."

Angie Howard crossed the tiny porch with a cup in her hand. Dressed in a pair of sweatpants and an old t-shirt, she squeezed onto the steps next to her husband. "My big butt takes up more room than yours."

"There's nothing wrong with your butt." Bennie nudged her with his shoulder and planted a kiss on her cheek. "You sleep okay?"

Angie drew in a long, slow breath, nodding. "I guess. Looks like you didn't, though."

"You noticed?"

She sipped her coffee and nodded. Wrapping her hands around the cup, she stared into the shadows draped across their neighbor's house, cast by a massive Pecan tree in their front yard. "Everything okay?"

Bennie nodded.

"You sure?"

Bennie nodded again. "I guess it's just nerves, you know."

"The new job?"

"I suppose."

Angie leaned against him. "I'm sure you'll do fine. You're a smart man. You'll pick it up fast, I bet."

Bennie finished what was left of his coffee and set the cup aside. One hand snaked beneath Angie's arm, his hand found her thigh and patted it.

"Thank you."

She withdrew slightly, surprised. "For what?"

"You know, everything. Footing the bills and all that."

Angie shrugged. "I use the electricity too, you know."

"Still." Bennie gripped her thigh and leaned into her. "I know it's been hard on you. I mean, all of it. Even when I was making money, I was gone all the time." He sighed. "You're a good woman."

Angie laughed. "What did you have in that cup?"

"It was coffee before you snuck up on me."

"I just walked outside. You must have been in some deep thought."

Bennie shrugged. "Nothing. Everything. I don't know."

Angie sighed, her hand rubbing his back. "I know this has been hard on you, too."

Bennie shrugged. The truth was that he was embarrassed. He'd failed in front of the world, more importantly, in front of his wife.

"When I first met you, I thought you were just some party guy, you know. The long hair, the leather pants —"

Bennie's laugh interrupted her. "Ugh. The leather pants."

"I know, right?" she agreed. "But anyway, I thought you were just another guitar player in just another band. I mean, y'all were good an all…"

Bennie nodded. "Like countless other bands, we weren't good enough."

Angie rubbed his back and sighed. "I don't think that's it. Y'all worked hard, traveled, did all the things you were supposed to. That one big break just never came. Bad luck, I guess."

Bennie nodded. "There were times when it was close, you know. We'd be piled up sleeping in Joe's van or some dive hotel, and everyone would be passed out or just asleep. I lay there and wrack my brain for something to push us over that hump, you know. We just needed that one big break and we'd've been set."

"Yeah," Angie said, nodding. "It's a big step, though. Most people don't make it over it."

"True," Bennie sighed. "Sometimes it just hurts because I wonder what if, you know."

"That's a big question. What if? I mean, doesn't everybody think that?"

Bennie nodded, casting his eyes toward the lightening sky. A sense of dread swamped him again. "I feel like today will change everything."

"Why? Do you feel like you're giving up? Because that's not it, sweetheart. I mean, you've worked regular jobs before."

"I know. I don't know what it is. I feel like today is different."

Angie sipped her coffee and watched two cars pass on the street. "Maybe it is. Maybe today will be the start of something new."

Or the end, Bennie thought.

"But, in any event, I need to get ready for work." Angie stood, a hand lingering on his shoulder. "You coming?"

"I guess I'd better change pants."

Angie laughed. "You know, Ben, sometimes things happen for a reason. Even if we don't understand it now, someday we'll look back and understand."

"Do you believe that?" he asked, looking up at her.

Angie shrugged. "What choice do we have?"

———

Sitting behind the wheel, Bennie watched his wife walk away. His eyes followed her as she approached the keypad next to a set of double doors. She scanned her badge and offered a quick wave before ducking inside. He watched her through the glass until the color of her scrubs faded into the shadows.

The knot in his stomach that he'd been trying to ignore tightened. He sighed, shaking his head. The phone felt heavy as he picked it up. Fingers fumbled their way to his message app and opened it. Her name was the second on his list. His thumb touched the screen by her name, and their last conversation appeared:

Angie: "We need anything from the store?"

Him: "Idk. Milk, maybe."

Angie: "K."

Him: "U said to remind U about those things U need?"

Angie: "Lol. K. Thanks."

Staring at the phone, he shook his head. Wondered what to say. Finally, he settled for "love you, babe." He sent the message and sat waiting for a response. When none came, he typed, "Be careful today," and sent it.

A honk from a pewter Ford pick-up that now consumed his rearview mirror prompted him to move. He spared the glass doors one last glance and pulled away from the curb. If something happened today, at least their last texts wouldn't be about milk and tampons.

Already programmed into the navigation app, the white triangle at "Begin Route" blinked at him. His eyes narrowed. Had it always blinked? He banged the phone against the side of his leg and checked it again. The word "recalculating" appeared, then a spinning disk. Finally, it stopped, and the familiar blue line marking his route appeared.

Pulling away from the hospital, his eyes followed the line on his phone. It made crisp, definitive turns. Left out of the parking lot. Right. Another left. Every turn was a perfect ninety-degree angle along a perfect line until it stopped abruptly in the middle of town.

"C'mon," he complained. He had the address for the interview, but the company was in the Industrial Park, and he wasn't familiar with that part of town.

Driving with one hand, he balanced the phone on his leg and used his free hand to expand the screen. The image of buildings and streets came into view, the blue line dissecting the town with precision.

He centered the spot where the line stopped and expanded it further. The line stopped at the intersection of two roads. Squinting, he recognized the wider road. It was the main thoroughfare that split Souls Harbor. A wide four-lane highway, with both north and southbound lanes having their own bridge over the river. The other road, the one he'd be traveling on was 14th Street.

"Piece of junk," he complained, dropping the phone onto the passenger seat. He knew how to get close. He had time to feel his way along after that. Besides, Angie said this company was a "big outfit". It shouldn't be too hard to find.

---

"Boomer?" Bennie's brow furrowed as he read the name from the utility worker's hard hat. The guy was young and thin, his face scarred by acne. He whipped the black trash bag before him several times, filling it with air, then covered the orange diamond-shaped sign warning drivers of UTILITY WORK. When he was done, he looked up, his eyes locking on Bennie's.

The kid nodded, smiling as if he knew a secret.

Inside the car, Bennie raised two fingers from the steering wheel and gave a polite head nod. Intentionally breaking eye contact with the worker, Bennie turned his head.

A white SUV occupied the space beside him. They'd both been mired in the same traffic, trading positions with the same cars several times. The blonde in the passenger seat smiled at him. He smiled back. Both vehicles inched forward, then stopped again.

Hard hats moved around, hovering over the red sedan in front of him. They converged in a group. One turned to the sidewalk.

Turning back to the SUV with a sigh, Bennie found the woman staring at him. Her blue eyes were intent, drawn. Serious. The flirtatious sparkle was gone. She raised her left hand, the sun glinting off the diamond on her finger.

Bennie started to raise his hand in a wave, but stopped when the woman's hand rotated, revealing her palm. Her index finger curled downward, and one perfectly manicured fingernail tapped the glass three times.

His brow furrowed. She tapped the glass again, and he turned, following her gesture. He glanced at the sidewalk, assuming that she was pointing at something, but found only a crew of workers. Looking back, he found her eyes now fixed on the sidewalk. Her fingernail tapped the glass again, and a tiny web of cracks appeared. She tapped the glass again, and the web spread.

The world slowed to a crawl. Bennie looked back at the sidewalk. The workers were standing around some type of machine. Thick cables hung from the back, like a giant squid languishing on the beach. As he watched, one of the workers removed his hard hat. His long, sandy brown hair was marked by a depression where the strap had been. The worker turned and smiled at him.

The man's smile wasn't welcoming, but weird and a little uneasy. A yellow stain marred his front teeth, the effect of years of smoking. He looked like he'd just told a dirty joke to a preacher.

Bennie gasped as a flood of memories filled his mind at once. He saw the same guy blowing smoke at him. It came in a long plume, like a mini tornado, before billowing against his window. He stared at the man, frozen by confusion, as song lyrics began to play over the radio. "If the truth means it's over... I'd rather hear lies...'Cause I'm stuck in a prison...where dreams go to die."

His mind showed him a peace symbol on a field of black as the lyrics continued. "Some say it's hell. Others call it Hades... but all I know is my final ride... will be in a big black Mercedes."

Bennie slammed the car into gear and opened the door. The roar of the street hit him like a fist. Engines idled all around him; the scent was stronger than he'd expected. He grimaced and looked around.

On the sidewalk, a worker in a white hard hat was barking orders. The sound of countless black birds radiated from a tree in the courtyard across the street. The blonde in the SUV was having an animated conversation with the man driving. Through the spider web of cracks, he saw multiple versions of her hands as they moved through the air in front of her.

Bennie rounded the front of his car. On the sidewalk, the workers all stopped and stared at him. He searched their faces, but none were the man he'd seen. He scanned the area, finding a man in a yellow safety vest sprinting down the sidewalk, running away from them. His yellow hard hat lay on its top halfway between, still spinning. As he watched, the man cut the corner on the next block and disappeared behind a tall brick building.

"Excuse me, sir. We're about to clear the lane."

Shaking his head, Bennie looked around at the middle-aged man now standing beside him. A garden of wrinkles surrounded the eyes staring at him from beneath the white hard hat. Bennie raised a hand weakly, pointing in the direction the other man had gone.

"Look, sir. You need to get back in your car. We're about to open this lane."

Bennie nodded dumbly, sparing another glance down the sidewalk.

"Get back in your car, sir. You're holding up traffic." As if on cue, the car behind Angie's Camry blasted its horn. The man behind the wheel threw his hands into the air, giving him a dumbfounded look.

Bennie nodded and retreated to his car. Inside, the sound of the world faded to a low hum again. He put the car in gear and looked back at the utility workers. The man in the white hard hat gave Bennie a thumbs-up, then turned to his crew. One of them stepped to the edge of the curb and started waving traffic forward.

The brakes on Angie Howard's Camry squeaked as it came to a stop at the intersection. The car in front of Bennie, quicker to react to the worker's cue, skirted beneath the light just before it turned red.

Bennie settled into the seat, his eyes on the side mirror. Still shaken by the flood of strange memories, he watched the utility crew slowly disperse. Why did the man run away? The guy was in a full-on sprint, like he was running from the cops.

Hell, Bennie thought. Why was he staring at him in the first place? Surely, he was just one of hundreds of cars that had passed by. What was it about him?

Still, there was a familiarity to the guy, like he'd seen him before. Had he? Maybe. There was always some sort of work going on in town. Road workers, men pouring the concrete for sidewalks, men building the city. They were all just guys in yellow safety vests and different colored hard hats. Because of their nearly constant presence, those men were part of the background.

Like he'd soon be.

Bennie pushed a hand through his hair and sighed. Cross-traffic was slowing. The light would change soon. He could put this whole strange incident behind him.

Bennie lifted his phone. His eyes widened when he saw the blue line on his navigation app. It ended directly in front of him. His eyes narrowed. The light turned green. His foot sank on the gas pedal.

A flash of movement grabbed his attention. He looked to his left. The hood ornament of the Mercedes gleamed in the early morning sun, accentuated by the black hood.

The phone vibrated in Bennie's hand. A robotic female voice filled the car. "You have reached your destination."

# CHAPTER NINE

Carver watched the minutes tick by on the old digital alarm clock by his bed. 4:58. 4:59. 5:00. His hand shot out and silenced the alarm on the first buzz, but he didn't get up. He rolled over and looked at the woman in the bed next to him.

Facing away from him, her blond hair was all he could see in the semi-darkness. Her breaths were coming in easy, rhythmic waves. He watched the covers rise and fall, envious of her sleep. He'd been awake most of the night.

Carver sighed, having spent the last few hours trying to decipher the sense of dread he'd awakened with. A darkness seemed to hang over him, a pall that he couldn't understand. Yesterday was a good day. Last night they went out and enjoyed a few green beers to celebrate the holiday. She was in a good mood. They came back to his place and enjoyed a particularly rousing bout of sex.

Today, he had three new clients to meet, and he expected to land at least two of them. The preliminaries looked good. Profitable. All was well.

So why did he feel like doing anything else but going to the office? He considered waking Belinda just for the company, but resisted. She'd ask a bunch of questions he didn't have the answers to. If he told her how he felt, she'd start with that new age, holistic, karma crap she was into.

Propping on an elbow, he looked at her. She was a good woman. Not perfect, but neither was he. She never asked him for much, except for some of his time, and never asked him for money. She didn't need his money. She had her own place, a good job, and her own car. It was the first adult relationship he'd had that was anything close to equal.

He smiled, thinking that the only reason she'd put up with his crap was that she genuinely cared about him. She deserved to be treated better. Regrets from past relationships tried to surface, but he fought them, reminding himself that Belinda wasn't Sharon, or Carmen, or Julie. But she was paying their dues.

The body next to him stirred. He put a hand on her hip, and she rolled over. Rubbing one eye with a fist, she stifled a yawn. "Did you oversleep?"

"Na," he said. "Just laying here."

"Is everything okay?" she asked, blinking sleep from her eyes. "You never hit the snooze button."

"I'm not snoozing. I'm just laying here looking at you."

Belinda gave him a curious smile. "Okay." Her hand came up and felt his forehead. "You sick?" she asked with a chuckle, sliding closer.

"Why do you put up with me?" he asked quietly.

Belinda shrugged one shoulder. "I guess I like you a little bit."

Carver stared at her. "I know I'm not an easy person to be with sometimes."

"You're a guy," she said, rolling her eyes. "As far as guys go, you're a pretty good one." Her hand found his back, caressing it gently.

"I didn't get much sleep last night." He sat up in bed.

"Really?" she asked, pulling him back. He didn't resist, laying across the bed with his head resting on her stomach. "I'd think you were worn out." She smiled, raking her fingers through his hair.

"Hmm," he said, agreeing. Typically, sex and a few drinks would knock him out cold.

"You got something on your mind?"

"I don't know. Just thinking too much, I guess."

"Work?" she asked.

Carver shook his head. "Believe it or not, no."

"You want to talk about it?"

"That's just it, I don't really know what it is. Just a lot of stuff. Crap from when I was a kid, old girlfriends, you."

Her hand stopped suddenly, her fingers buried in his hair. "Me? I hope it was good."

"It was," he said with a smile. He sighed, staring up at the ceiling. The scant light from the bathroom nightlight painted it with long shadows. His eyes traced them as he considered his next words.

"I just feel weird, you know. I can't explain it because I don't understand it myself."

"Maybe the universe is trying to tell you something."

Carver groaned softly. "Don't do that. Please."

"What? I'm just saying." She went back to combing her fingers through his hair. "I know you don't go for all that stuff, but if you look into it, it makes a lot of sense."

"Crystals and the stars and all that? Really?"

"Not just that, sweetie. It's about the energy we create. There *is* science behind it. Everything in the universe has a certain energy. Some are good. Some are bad. That's why two people work well together and two others don't."

"Okay," he sighed.

"Look. All life on Earth is carbon-based. Scientists know this."

"And?"

"And carbon atoms have the fewest limitations and the most possible structures. Isn't that cool? All of us, everything that exists, is basically made of the same thing. It makes sense that everything would be connected. Don't you think?"

"I don't know about all that," he said, reaching back for her free hand. When she placed hers in his, he brought it around and laid it on his chest. "What I do know is that this is nice."

"It is," she said, giving him a quick squeeze. "I'm sure you'll probably say no, but I'm going to ask anyway. I'm off today. Why don't we spend the day together? Lay around, have a late breakfast. Maybe go for a walk." She chuckled. "Maybe even sneak back to bed for a little while."

Carver moaned. "That does sound nice."

"Really?" she asked, surprised. "You do know it's not the weekend, right?"

"I know what day it is." Carver ran his fingertip up and down her hand as his eyes went back to the ceiling. "The reason I couldn't sleep is that I had this strange feeling that I shouldn't go to work today. I laid here for hours arguing with myself, trying to figure out why I feel this way."

"Did you come up with anything?"

Carver sighed. "Not a damned thing."

"Well, why risk it? I mean, whether you're 'vibing' with the Earth's energy or not, you have to admit that it is odd for you. You're usually in a rush to get to work."

Carver grunted his agreement, or at least his refusal to argue the point. Belinda was right. He enjoyed his work, but it was also more than that. His success defined him; it was a middle finger in the face of all those rich snobs in law school, the ones who'd come from money.

"Everybody's heard about people who have a strange feeling about not getting on a plane, and then that plane crashes. I've seen it on the news. And that guy who went jogging instead of going to work on 9/11."

"I wouldn't say it's all that."

"Well," she leaned down and kissed the top of his head. "Either way, you deserve a day off, and this might just be the best reason you can get."

"I just…" Carver shook his head. "I mean, I can't…"

"You argue with yourself a minute, hun. I have to pee, and you laying on my bladder ain't helping one bit." She slid from beneath Carver's head, putting a pillow in her place.

He watched her until she disappeared through the

bathroom door. Her hips moved well beneath the long t-shirt, stirring his desire. Her legs, still holding onto the glimpse of the summer's tan, moved effortlessly. Her thighs just brushed one another as she moved.

"You know," she called through the open doorway. "You *are* the boss. It's not like you're going to get canned if you call in every once in a while."

"I have appointments."

"Reschedule them."

"It's not that easy."

"Good morning, Mrs. Johnson," Belinda said, her voice deepened in a poor imitation of him. "Carver here. Reschedule all my appointments for today. I'm going to spend the day with my beautiful and exceedingly brilliant girlfriend. What's that? Why yes, I am a lucky man. Very lucky indeed."

"Is that supposed to be me?" he asked with a laugh. "Because it sounds more like Goofy."

The toilet flushed, and Belinda peeked through the door as she washed her hands, "If the oversized shoe fits..." she said with a laugh.

"Wow. You're awake ten minutes and already going for the throat. Glad you don't work for the insurance companies."

Belinda shared his laugh as she exited the bathroom, tossing the towel back onto the counter. "I could never be a lawyer," she said, crawling back into bed beside him. "My memory sucks. I could never remember all those case files and stuff."

Carver grunted. "To be honest, interns and junior lawyers do most of the work, researching cases and all that. I just provide the image and showmanship. It's all about the confidence you project."

"Is that what you're doing now?" she asked quietly, one eyebrow arching slightly as she looked at him.

Carver looked at her for a moment, then shrugged.

"I know you, Carver Willis. Something has knocked you a

little off kilter. I can see it in your eyes. It's not much, just enough for you to notice. And —" she pointed a finger at him, "You don't have a clue how to handle it."

Carver shook his head as Belinda got back into bed, lying next to him. "I don't know what it is. Maybe I'm just having a stroke."

Belinda laughed. "No such luck. The universe is trying to tell you something, hun. You just don't want to hear it."

"What am I supposed to do? Should I just call in and tell everyone I got a bad feeling? Then what am I going to do when one of them calls me and says, 'My gut is telling me to stay home today.' He shook his head. 'Sorry, Boss, my shockrums are out of whack.' It'd be a cluster…"

"It's chakra," Belinda corrected with a grin, rubbing his chest. "Look, you do what you want to do, sweetheart. I'm just telling you what's going on. You may be a hotshot lawyer and all, but this is my department."

"How do you know it's not just indigestion?"

"Does it feel like indigestion?"

Carver sighed. "No," he said reluctantly. "It doesn't."

"This is the last I'll say about it. You make a living trusting your instincts. Why not do it now?"

*Trust your gut, Carver. Always trust your gut.*

Carver laughed. "You're good. You know that?"

Belinda breathed on her fingernails and polished them on her shirt. "I just do what I can with what I have." She rolled on her side, sliding closer to him. Carver's hand instantly went to her thigh as she threw one leg across him.

"I must admit, spending the day with you does sound inviting." His hand slid up and down the supple skin of her leg. "To hell with it. I'll tell Jean I'm sick."

"Yippee," Belinda said with a smile.

Carver looked at her, found genuine happiness in her eyes, and smiled. He'd dated lots of women, married one, and slept with his share, but he rarely ever saw one so content to just be with him.

"You should always trust your gut."

*Always trust your gut, Carver. Always.*

Carver's smile faded. Had he ever told Belinda about that day with his mother? He didn't remember, but he did tend to ramble when he was drunk. He might have.

"How about you make coffee, and I'll run through the shower." Belinda giggled. "Today is going to be a great day, you wait and see."

"I hope you're right. You know I'll just have to work that much harder tomorrow to catch up."

"Don't be such a fuddy-duddy. Let tomorrow worry about itself. I'll be in the shower."

Carver shrugged as Belinda clambered off the bed, slapping her butt as she went past. "Maybe I'll join you."

Belinda stopped in the bathroom doorway, leaning against it as she raised one leg behind her. "Come on, lover boy. We can get clean, then get dirty again."

Carver sat up and pushed himself off the bed with a grunt. "Let me just call Jean. I'll be in in a sec." He picked up his cell phone from the bedside table, but almost dropped it when it started vibrating in his hand. The knot in his stomach tightened as he answered it.

"Mister Willis? Carver Willis?"

"Yes," he said, answering the male voice on the other end of the phone. "Who is this? Can I help you?"

"This is Officer Aaron Rogers, Souls Harbor P.D. Do you own the building at 2314 Jamison Street?"

"Yes, I do. It's my law office. Is there a problem?"

"I'd say so, sir. I am currently watching water pour from beneath your front door. I'm no plumber, but I'd say you've got a sizeable leak."

"Holy shit. Dammit."

"If you give us permission, we'd be happy to shut the water off, though I don't know how much good it'll do now. Looks like it's been at it a while."

"Yes, yes," Carver mumbled, his eyes going to the open bathroom door. He listened to the sound of the shower running and shook his head with a sigh. "If you don't mind. I'll be in shortly."

"No problem. Glad to help. Thank you."

"Yeah, thanks." Carver's hand fell to his side as he ended the call. "Damn," he said to the empty room. He walked to the bathroom door. "Hey, babe."

Poking her head out of the shower, Belinda's smile faded when she saw Carver's face. "No. Carver. Really?"

"The police just called."

"The police?" Belinda's eyes widened. "That's never good."

"Tell me about it. Apparently, the office is flooded. A water leak of some kind. A major one from the sound of it."

"Aw. I'm sorry."

"The cops are going to shut the water off, but I have to go in. I'm going to have to call my insurance agent, a plumber, and God knows who else. Reschedule everybody."

"I'm so sorry. Want me to go with you? Maybe we can salvage some of the day."

"Nah," Carver sighed. "I'm sure this crap will keep me busy most of the day. You'd just be bored stiff waiting around."

Belinda ducked her head back inside the curtain. "You know, if they've shut the water off, you have a little time…"

"I wish I could. I really do, but I can't even think about anything until I get this crap fixed. There are tons of files. The office will be out of commission for no telling how long. I've got to find an alternate site. It's going to be a nightmare."

"Okay then. Go. I know you've got to handle things," she said from behind the curtain. "I'm almost done. I'll be ready to go in a few."

Carver waved a hand at the curtain. "No. Take your time. Stay as long as you need to."

Belinda poked her head out of the shower again. "Really?"

"Yes," he said, nodding. "Don't make a thing out of it, okay?" He moved in and kissed her lips. "I've got to go."

"Be careful, hun." Belinda waited for his response, but none came. Smiling, she stepped beneath the hot water. He'd said not to make it a thing, but it was. It was the first time he'd ever let her stay while he went to work. It might not have been "a thing" to him, but it was a big thing to her.

———

Brian Sandel talked almost the entire commute, filling Carver's Mercedes with his usual deep, monotonous voice. He read stock report after stock report, but Carver barely heard any of it. His mind was racing with remedies for the current catastrophe. If the floors were ruined, they'd have to be replaced. That would take weeks. He'd have to find a temporary office space, move tons of files. He'd have to deal with plumbers, floor installers, and his insurance company. They'd probably find asbestos and lead and mold, and no telling what else. The whole thing could end up costing a fortune.

He took the long sweeping curve into town with a heavy sigh. Getting a slightly later start, he'd expected traffic to be murder but was pleasantly surprised. There had only been one car at the stop sign on Fourteen. The traffic on Highway Eleven was moving briskly. He'd end up at the office at his regular time, more or less.

He breezed beneath the first green light, then the second. As he neared the third signal, his eyes drifted to his left. A man wearing a dark suit and a maroon shirt was sitting on the steps of a vacant building. He looked up, watching as the black Mercedes passed beneath the light.

Carver spared him a glance over his shoulder. The guy

looked vaguely familiar, and he wondered if he was a lawyer. Maybe he'd been the opposing counsel on a case?

When Carver looked back around, the traffic light ahead of him was turning yellow. His foot sank on the accelerator. The car responded immediately, surging forward. The brake lights on the car in front of him glared. He checked his mirror and changed lanes in one action.

The light turned red.

Carver barreled through it and into the side of a silver Camry. For the briefest of seconds before the impact, he saw the face of the driver, a man younger than him with sandy brown hair. His eyes grew wide with shock, but also a knowing. He looked almost as if he'd expected this to happen.

The sound of metal crunching filled Carver's ears, then his mother's voice. *Always trust your gut, baby. Always.* His hands clenched on the steering wheel. And then there was darkness.

# CHAPTER TEN

Angie Howard's hand reached across the bed, searching blindly for her husband's body. Finding the space next to her empty, she raised her head from the pillow. Sleepy eyes struggled to focus in the dim light. Rolling over, she checked her phone plugged next to the bed. Squinting as light erupted into the dark room, she stared at the cracked screen in disbelief. 4:11 A.M. Why was Bennie up so early?

Her eyes went to the window. Outside, the sky was still black, but sunrise wasn't far off. Laying down with a sigh, she debated getting another hour of sleep or checking on her husband.

After her mind played a multitude of scenarios that would explain Bennie's absence, none of them good, she threw the covers back with a groan. Sitting up on the bed, she rubbed her eyes and looked at the bathroom door. There was no sliver of light coming from beneath it, dashing her hopes that he'd just gotten up to pee.

She stood and yawned, stretching as she rounded the bed in a long nightshirt and short socks. Bennie had an interview with a construction company today. She hoped he wasn't having second thoughts. They needed the money.

Angie passed through a darkened living room and into the kitchen. The smell of coffee hung in the air, but there was no sign of Bennie. She poured herself a cup, added two sugars and a touch of milk, then checked the front door. Tiptoeing to look through the small diamond-shaped window, she found her husband sitting on the steps.

As she watched him gently strum his guitar, a pang of guilt washed through her. He was good at it, but not great. Although he had hopes of making it big, she doubted he ever would. His band had enjoyed some success, moving above the local dives and back road honkytonks to bigger venues, but that was it. But even that didn't earn them enough money for Bennie to avoid having to work odd jobs between gigs.

Still, he wanted it so badly. So many times he'd told her that playing in a band was what he was born to do. When his band fell apart, he'd taken it hard. She knew he was fighting depression, and her heart ached for him, but the bills still had to be paid. Yes, he had an artist's soul, but the power company didn't care about that. The rent couldn't be paid in hopes and dreams. They wanted money, and right now that was in short supply.

Angie opened the door and stepped out into the cool of the new day. "You're up early."

Bennie jumped, spilling coffee down his right leg. "Damn. You scared me," he said, wiping the leg of his jeans. "I thought you'd sleep another hour at least."

"I rolled over and you weren't there."

Bennie smiled, giving her a quick kiss as she joined him on the concrete steps. Together, they watched a pickup truck roll past on the street in front of them. Tools rattled in the bed when it hit the pothole in front of their mailbox.

"So?" Angie asked, cradling the cup with both hands. "Couldn't sleep, huh?"

Bennie shook his head. "I've been up a while. I don't know what it is."

"Nervous about the interview?"

Bent over the guitar on his lap, Bennie shrugged. "I don't know. Maybe."

Angie's brow furrowed. "You're still going, aren't you?"

"Yeah," Bennie said, strumming the guitar softly. "We need the money, right?"

"It would definitely help out."

"Then it's settled." Bennie tightened the G string on

his guitar and checked the sound. Nodding, he went back to strumming.

"You don't sound too excited. You know, Daddy said it's a big outfit. Lots of room for advancement."

"I know. You've told me twice already."

Angie shrugged one shoulder and sipped her coffee. Sitting quietly, listening to him strum his guitar, a strange awkwardness rose between them. There was a hint of resentment in his voice that she didn't like. Surely, he didn't blame her for their situation. Her salary was the only thing keeping a roof over their heads.

"Tell me lies, make me believe," Bennie sang, almost in a whisper. "In the innocence of babies. Cause the only thing I can see…is that death rides in a Mercedes."

"That's dark," Angie said with a chuckle.

Bennie shrugged one shoulder. "It's just stupid stuff I do. I just clear my mind and sing whatever comes to me, you know."

"Still."

"Well, it is early." Bennie set the guitar aside and turned to his wife. "I've been doing this for hours, and it always comes back to some version of the same few lines. Babies, lies, death, and a Mercedes. It's weird."

"We don't know anybody who drives a Mercedes, do we?"

"I don't."

"It's really dark, Ben. Death in a Mercedes. I don't like it."

"Well, it doesn't matter now anyway, does it?"

"What does that suppose to mean?" she asked.

"I just mean if I take this job, none of it will matter. I won't have time to do anything else, really."

"It's eight hours a day, Bennie."

"I know. I mean, at first, I'm sure I'll play and maybe even write some new stuff. After a while, I'll move on, and eventually, I won't even pick up a guitar. One day, years from now, I'll stumble across it in a closet and remember that once upon a time I could play."

"You're being a little dramatic, don't you think?"

"No. And I think you know it too."

Angie sighed. "What else can we do?"

Bennie shrugged, clasping his hands between his knees as he watched a car roll past their cracked driveway. "Why don't we just leave?"

"Leave?"

"You know, pack our crap in the car and just go. We could travel around and play gigs as we find them. Think about it, no rent, no bills."

"Where would we live? In the car?"

"Sure. Why not?"

Angie sighed and pushed her hand through her hair. "Bennie, you know I love you, and I do believe in your dream. I really do. But we have to face facts."

"Facts?" he asked. "What facts?"

"Well, we're not kids anymore. When we were, it was fine sleeping wherever and just wandering around playing music. That was great...back then."

"But not now?"

"We're both approaching forty, Bennie. We're not irresponsible kids anymore. Sleeping in the car would probably kill both our backs. I mean, I have a good job. We should be thinking about the future."

Bennie grunted. "Kids and a white picket fence and all that, huh?"

"I didn't say that, but..."

"But nothing. Is that what you want? Go to work and come home, tend to kids. Pay bills. Maybe go out to eat on the weekend if we can afford a babysitter and dinner? Grind it out for some rich guy and be thankful for the meager pittance he gives us on Fridays?"

"That's life, Bennie. It's what people do."

Bennie grunted. "Why? Because that's what the world

tells us we should do?"

Angie threw her hands up and let them drop. "Because that's what normal people do."

"Normal people?" Bennie asked, searching her eyes for something, though he didn't know what. "Is that all there is? Really? We toil away at a job for thirty years and then have kids so they can do the same thing? Doesn't it seem at least a little bit like a circle of discontentment?"

"Circle of discontentment? What?" Angie sighed. "I don't know, Bennie. Existential angst aside, people have to eat. We have got to have shelter. I mean, those are basic human needs, and they cost money. Short of robbing banks or scamming little old ladies out of their social security checks, it's the only way I know to make money."

Bennie laced his fingers behind his neck and let his head fall back with a groan. "I get all that. It just seems like a shitty way to spend what little time we have here on Earth, you know." He dropped his hands, taking hers in his. "Think about this. What if money wasn't an issue? What would you do? What makes you happy?"

"I don't know. I never really thought about it, Bennie."

"We were really happy when we first met."

Angie laughed. "We were dumb kids. I mean, we drank and smoked so much pot that we probably fried some part of our brains."

"But we were *happy*."

"Yes," she said with a smile and a nod. "We were. I'll give you that. My parents weren't, but we were."

"Just think, baby. We could travel. See the country. Remember when you used to sing with me? Everybody said you were good."

"Jesus, Bennie. That was sitting in a parking lot in the back of a junked-up van. And everybody was stoned."

"Still."

"Still nothing. I could never get on stage, and I'm pretty sure that if I got that drunk and stoned, my body would probably just shut down. We're not spring chickens anymore, Babe."

Bennie released her hands. Turning, he picked up his guitar and put it on his knee. "C'mon, babe. Let's hear it."

"No." Angie shook her head. "It'll be embarrassing."

"Nobody's here but me." Bennie nudged her with his shoulder. "C'mon."

"Bennie, stop. I need to start getting ready for work."

"C'mon, babe. Just try. A few lines."

"I don't want to."

Bennie's shoulders drooped. "What if the doctor told you that you had six months to live, Ange? Would you chase your dreams then?"

"Bennie, look." She snaked an arm around his waist. "I know you're anxious and that the band breaking up was hard on you. I really do. I get that, but you're comparing getting a regular job to a death sentence, and I just can't buy it."

"That's not it at all."

"Then what is it?" she asked.

"I don't know." Benny pushed both hands through his hair. "I woke up like that—" he snapped his fingers. "My heart was racing, I was sweating. To be honest, I felt like I was about to scream."

"What?" Her hand found his forehead. "Are you sick?"

"No. I feel fine except for this weird thing I got going on. I feel like something's going to happen today. I don't know what, but I feel like it might be bad."

"Maybe you're just anxious about the interview."

Bennie shook his head. "I don't think that's it. I mean, I've interviewed for more important stuff than this. I don't know what it is."

"If you're not sick, that's all it could be. Maybe all this stuff you've been dealing with is coming out like that. Did you have a nightmare or something?"

Bennie shrugged. "I don't remember one."

"Then that's just it, Bennie. You've gotten yourself all worked up. It's just nerves." She rubbed his back and then used his shoulder to push up from the steps.

"Where are you going?"

"I told you. I'm going to have breakfast and then get ready for work."

"Just like that? Everything I said is just brushed away like an afterthought."

"No," she said, standing on the porch looking down at him. "I don't know what else to say. I don't think there's a right answer here, Ben. All I know is that if I don't get to work, then we'll be eating instant noodles all week, and those things hurt my stomach."

Bennie waved a hand at her. "Fine then."

"What do you want me to say, Bennie? You had a bad dream, you're nervous about the new job."

"I mean the other stuff?"

"About us just up and becoming wandering singers?" She laughed. "Surely you weren't serious."

"I guess not," Bennie said, deflated. He was as serious as a heart attack, but knew there was no sense pleading his case further. Angie had dismissed it as foolish and irresponsible with a wave of her hand. In her mind, it was over and done.

Angie mussed his hair. "C'mon. Let's have breakfast. I'll make you the last two eggs."

"That sounds good," Bennie lied, forcing a smile. He didn't want the last two eggs. He didn't want to eat at all. He watched Angie walk into the house, then picked up the mug beside him. What little coffee left in it had gotten cold. He tossed it into the yard with a grunt.

Standing, he grabbed his guitar by the neck and looked at it. For so long, this had been the tool he thought would make his living using. Today, that would probably change. Shaking his head, he looked at the open front door. The sound of Angie in the kitchen came not so gently to the porch.

*If the truth means it's over, then please tell me lies.*

―――――

Bennie sat in his wife's car, brooding. His eyes were fixed on the red light in front of him, but his mind was miles away. Their drive had been quiet. The squeaky voice of the latest pop sensation coming from the speakers filled most of the time between their house and the hospital. Angie liked the band. To him, it was sickening. The music was canned, the lyrics sophomoric.

The worst part was knowing whoever the guy singing was, he probably had the latest slick haircut and a million bucks in the bank. It was all so unfair. Some kid bebops onto the scene and boom, he's a star, while he'd spent years paying his dues, only to end up interviewing for a construction job. Talent and hard work meant nothing anymore. It was all about your looks and catching on with the teenage crowd.

After dropping Angie off at the hospital, he'd spend the rest of the drive lost in thought, moving along with traffic in an almost unconscious will. By the time he stopped at the light, marred in traffic, he'd traced all his recent failures back to one event. He'd passed on the chance to move the band to L.A. Though no one came out and said it, he knew that was the beginning of the end. And he was the main holdout. For Angie.

Of course, hindsight was twenty-twenty. He'd been so in love with her. She was as important to him as the music. She didn't want to move, forcing him to make a choice. He'd chosen her, and the hope of finding a workaround.

Bennie's chest rose and fell in frustrated pants. It would be easy to blame everything on Angie, but it was his choice. But if only she'd gone with them. His songs might be on the radio now. They might have a nice house and fancy cars. Back then, she said she didn't need all those things. Now, however, he wondered if she wanted them.

The honk of a horn snatched Bennie from his thoughts. He glanced back at the white SUV behind him. The man driving was waving his hand around above the steering wheel while talking to the woman in the seat next to him. She was looking out the passenger side window, uninterested.

Bennie tossed his hands into the air. The signal had turned green, but his lane of traffic was blocked all the way to the light. The other two lanes were creeping forward, but they too soon came to a stop.

Over the top of the car in front of him, he caught sight of the tip of an orange road sign and groaned. The reason for the delay was more than just congestion. He checked his side mirror, hoping for a chance to merge, but traffic was at a standstill. He closed his eyes in a frustrated sigh and leaned back into the seat.

Pushing his hands through his hair, he gathered it at the nape of his neck, pulling it through his fist. When the hair dropped out of his grasp sooner than he expected, he dropped his hands to his lap. It was just one more sign that things had changed, probably forever.

Watching the cars beyond the light slowly shuffle themselves, making room in his lane, the notion of turning right crept into his mind. He could turn right, go four blocks, take a left, and head to the interstate. I-22 would take him south, then he could make the connection headed west. He could be in California in five or six days. Maybe less if he drove hard and didn't stop too much.

His eyes darted to the gas gauge. Less than half a tank. That and the twelve dollars in his pocket wouldn't get him far. His foot lifted from the brake, and he rolled through the intersection just as the light turned red. Coming to a stop behind a red Chevrolet, he waited with everyone else.

Benny moaned, instantly regretting his decision. Even if he didn't go to the interstate, he could have turned right and avoided the stalled traffic. Rubbing his eye with his left hand, he admonished himself for being so distracted.

Leaning to his right, he could see the orange sign proclaiming Utility Work. Three cars up, several hard hats bobbed around in his lane. The faint sound of equipment wove its way to him among the sounds of impatient drivers.

Checking his side mirror, he watched the white SUV nose its way into the next lane, using size and muscle to procure the spot. When it rolled up and stopped next to him, the blonde in the passenger seat met his eyes. The faintest of smiles tugged at the corners of her maroon lips.

Bennie smiled back at her, adding a quick nod. The man just past her was still waving his hands around, probably complaining about the traffic. When the driver leaned forward, looking around the woman and directly at him, Bennie looked away.

The hard hats had converged at one point. Three of them disappeared as their wearers stooped. They reappeared for a few seconds, then disappeared again. The ones he could see were moving to the side of the road.

A man appeared on the sidewalk. His yellow hard hat perched atop a long crop of stringy hair. He was unshaven and didn't look like he'd slept well. The man stopped suddenly, then turned and started walking along the sidewalk toward Bennie.

A sense of recognition struck him like a bolt of lightning. Bennie stared at the man's face, sure that he knew him from somewhere, but couldn't recall where. With each step the man took, the sense of familiarity grew. The guy was tall and lean. He raised the cigarette held between the first two fingers of his right hand. The ember blazed. The man blew smoke out his nose.

His eyes met Bennie's, and he stopped suddenly. Bennie stared back at the man, now even with his passenger-side window. The shock wore off quickly, and the man offered him a quick head nod.

A horn honked, and Bennie's head snapped around. The man in the white SUV was getting angry, motioning violently at the cars ahead of him. Bennie looked at the woman. She shrugged one shoulder, raising her eyebrows as they rolled forward.

Bennie looked around, noticing that the cars ahead of him were moving. He spared the worker another glance, but he'd gone to collect the sign. His foot lifted from the brake, and he inched forward with the other drivers. Nearing the intersection, the Chevrolet sped up and skirted beneath a yellow light. It turned red before Bennie could do the same.

Stopped at the light, he checked his side mirror again. The man had laid the sign aside and was standing with the group. Everyone was either talking amongst themselves or checking on the foreign-looking piece of equipment. Except for the man he thought he knew. He was standing with his hard hat at his side, the cigarette held to his lips pinched by his thumb and pointer finger.

He lowered the cigarette, revealing a grin. His lips puckered slightly and produced a plume of smoke. The smoke quickly closed the distance between them and billowed against his window. Bennie recoiled, shocked.

When the smoke cleared, he saw the man in the mirror walking toward him. Bennie's brow furrowed. "What the hell, dude?" he asked, almost in a whisper. His heart began to race. Suddenly, he didn't want anything to do with the guy. He might have seen him before, but he wasn't a friend. There was an odd look in his eyes, a look that Bennie didn't like.

He checked the light. It was still red. He eased the car forward a few inches before checking the mirror again. The guy had closed half the distance between them but had stopped. His eyes narrowed as the dirty hand holding the cigarette rose slowly.

Bennie watched intently, unable to look away. The cigarette moved in the man's grasp, manipulated by fingers used to the action. His middle finger coiled behind the butt, holding it to his thumb. With little effort, he thumped it toward Bennie's car. It left his thumb and began to tumble through the air. The center of the filter was stained like an old bruise. The ember on the other end was nothing but gray ash. In the mirror, the cigarette grew as it came toward him.

*Objects in the mirror may be closer than they appear.*

The cigarette butt flipped end over end in a perfect arch. He saw the filter again. The entire filtered end was a stain. Then the ember. The movement through the air had given it a spark of life. Cracks of red glowed through the gray ash.

The butt struck the mirror in an explosion of tiny sparks. Bennie jumped, his head snapping around to check the light. His heart pounded in his chest. Sweat collected at his temples.

Cross traffic was slowing. His light turned green an instant later. Bennie stomped the gas, and Angie's Camry leaped forward. Movement caught his eye. He turned to his left in time to see the shiny grill of a black car bearing down on him.

In the blink of an eye, his brain had time to process one thought before his world turned black. *Make me believe with the innocence of babies…because all I can see is that death drives a big black Mercedes.*

# CHAPTER ELEVEN

Carver Willis strode into his home office dressed in a plain white T-shirt and a pair of boxer shorts. Squinting as the flip of a switch flooded the room with bright light, he went immediately to his desk. He nudged the padded chair aside with his leg, sending it rolling into the wall. Snatching the middle drawer open, he grabbed a pen and a yellow legal pad.

The legal pad dropped to the desk on top of the open case file he'd been reviewing last night while waiting for Belinda to get dressed for dinner. The disturbance sent a ripple through the half-inch of melted ice in the bottom of the crystal tumbler next to it, also left over from last night. He'd been working on his second drink when Belinda showed up. Typically, he resented being interrupted, but the slinky black dress she wore changed his mind.

Not bothering to sit, he picked up a pen and stared down at the paper. Two hours ago, he'd awakened with the incessant need to write something down, but couldn't remember what. Something important. Something vital.

His eyes went to the pen in his hand. It was a fancy one. A gift from one of the clients he'd successfully represented. Right now, he couldn't remember which one. There were so many clients and so many pen sets. Apparently, expensive pens were the gift du jour when your attorney gets you a boatload of money.

His free hand came up and rubbed his forehead, finding it damp with sweat. He shook his head and looked at the pen again, willing it to write the thing that his mind couldn't remember. When nothing happened, he growled and tossed the pen onto the pad.

Retrieving the chair, he pulled it to the desk and sat

down with a sigh. He hated not being able to remember things. Normally, his memory was excellent. He could remember cases, clients, situations, addresses, and birthdays. But not this. This one thing, whatever it was, remained just out of his mental grasp. It fluttered in his mind like a moth in the night.

Carver picked up the pen again and leaned over the pad. His eyes went to the pen again, but closed after a few seconds of inactivity. He took a deep breath and released it slowly, calming his mind. Belinda had once told him about transcendental meditation. At the time, he thought it was mostly bullshit, but after hours of trying to remember, he was willing to give anything a shot. He'd never be able to relax until he got it out.

Another deep breath came and went. Then another. As he exhaled the third breath, his hand began to quiver slightly. He dared not open his eyes.

Another deep breath came and went, and his hand began to move. He opened his eyes in the excitement, and his hand stopped. Carver grunted and pulled the chair closer with his foot. He sat down and closed his eyes again, resuming his deep breaths. After three breaths, his hand began to move again.

This time, he kept his eyes closed, allowing his hand to scribble what it wanted. One short word, then his hand slid down to another line. Another short word. Was it the same as the first? His hand dropped down again. This time, he followed the tip of the pen in his mind as it rolled smoothly across the page. It was a short word, all lowercase letters in cursive.

Greed? he thought, his brow furrowing deeply. His hand dropped down again. A fourth word. This one was different. A little longer, but also in lowercase cursive. His hand moved down again, wrote a short word, then stopped. Carver waited, working hard to keep his mind clear. After a few seconds, his hand moved down again and began to write. This word was larger, printed in capital letters. In his mind, he could see the ballpoint rolling against the page. The tip of the pen pressed into the paper. Ink transferred to the page.

When his hand stopped, Carver sat motionless. He waited patiently despite his eagerness to see what he'd written. He wanted the complete message.

After several moments of inactivity, he opened his eyes. Staring at the page, his brow creased. His head tilted slightly as he looked at the words.

green

green

green

silver

BLACK

"What the hell?" Carver dropped the pen and lifted the pad. He leaned back in the chair as his free hand scratched the back of his head. His eyes roved over the collection of words, trying to make sense of them. Were they part of a message? A song? Maybe a nursery rhyme.

His mind catapulted him back to his youth. He was lying in bed, his mother sitting beside him. She couldn't carry a tune in a bucket, but she'd sung to him when he was young. His lips were pulled into a half smile by the memory.

The moment slipped away when his eyes focused on the words again. The repetition lent itself to a nursery rhyme, but if it was, it wasn't any he'd ever heard. "Green, green, green, silver...black!" He sang in a whisper, putting an emphasis on the last word. When the lyrics failed to jog his memory, he shook his head and dropped the tablet to his desk.

Rubbing his eyes with his fingertips, he stifled a yawn. This, he thought, is what woke me up so early? It's utter nonsense. Standing, he put a hand on either side of the pad and stared down at it.

"What a load of crap."

Carver scratched his backside as he rounded the desk. Since he was up, he might as well have a cup of coffee. Halfway to the door, a "poof" stopped him in his tracks. He turned, his eyes bulging when he saw flames dancing along the notepad he'd just been holding.

"Holy shit!" He hurried back to his desk, looking for something to extinguish the flames. He grabbed the glass next to the pad and doused the flames. The scrap of water had little effect on the flames except to change their color from white to blue for one brief instant.

"Shit," he grumbled. Grabbing a letter opener, he drug the pad over the edge of his desk and onto the floor, sparing the case file beneath. Without thinking, he began to stomp the papers with his bare feet.

He let out a sigh of relief when the flames disappeared. He bent with a groan and lifted the pad. Holding it before him, he tilted it to the side, watching the last few scraps of charred paper slide from the pad and flutter to the floor like black snowflakes. His eyes followed them all the way to the hardwood.

Looking back at the pad, his eyes narrowed. The pages beneath the one he'd written on were untouched by the flames, marred only by smears of soot. Halfway down the page, he saw a big blob of soot and four smaller ones—his partial footprint. Probing the paper with his fingertip, his brow furrowed deeply. The page wasn't even warm.

"Damn," he sighed. "That's crazy." Shaking his head, he eyed the pad. How did it suddenly catch fire? And moreover, how could one page be reduced to ashes while the one beneath it wasn't even scorched?

He rubbed his left eye with his free hand. This morning was shaping up to be a real pisser, and he hadn't even had his coffee yet.

He tossed the pad back onto his desk with a sigh and started out of the room. Stopping at the door, he looked back over his shoulder at the smeared page of the legal pad. Striding back to his desk, he grabbed the pad and took it with him. If it happened again, he didn't want to risk burning the house down.

———

Carver flipped the switch on as he entered, flooding the bedroom in bright light. "Hey, Babe, get a load of this," he said, flopping down on the bed beside Belinda. "You'll never believe this crap."

Belinda groaned and pulled a pillow over her head. "What time is it?"

"I know, it's early. But check this out. C'mon." He shook her hip with his free hand, leaving a black smudge on the covers. "Check this crap out."

Belinda dragged the pillow off her face and sat up. "A legal pad?" she asked, shaking her head. "Fascinating."

"No. I mean, yes, it's a legal pad, but that's not it. Look at this." He thrust the charred edge of the top page toward her.

Belinda rubbed her eye with a fist, squinted at the pad, and shook her head again. "What am I supposed to be looking for?"

"This." Carver fingered the edge, sending a flurry of charred paper onto the sheets. When he wiped them away, they left long black streaks on the fabric.

"Carver, you're making a mess. What did you do?" Belinda wiped the streaks, but they weren't going anywhere. She looked up at Carver. "Are you smoking again?"

"No," he said. The truth was that he did occasionally get a craving, but that didn't count. He tapped the face of the pad with his fingertip. "The paper burned up by itself."

Belinda rubbed her face again and scratched her head as her groggy mind tried to process what she was hearing. She looked at him. Her brow creased. Her head fell to one side. "What?"

"Just what I said. Just poof. See?" He shook the pad, losing more ashes onto the sheets.

"Okay," Belinda took the pad from his hand and held it flat to stop the ashes from falling. "You're going to ruin the sheets, Babe."

"I don't care about the sheets," Carver said, standing. "I thought I was losing my mind, but there is the proof."

"Proof of what?" Belinda gently touched the charred edge of the first sheet of paper. She rubbed the ash between her thumb and index finger. "Why did you burn it?"

"That's just it." Carver came back to the bed but didn't sit. "I woke up early this morning with this notion that I needed to write something down. I thought maybe something for a case or something. I went into my office and got this pad, but nothing came."

Belinda's left eyebrow arched slowly as she watched Carver pace.

"Then I did that meditation thing where you just clear your mind and wham!"

"It caught on fire?"

"No. Not then, but I began to write something down."

"What?"

Carver stopped suddenly, scratching his chin as he thought. "Damn. I can't remember now. Something green. Maybe. Damn."

"And then it burned up?"

"Yes. Exactly. I wrote it down and then, poof. It burned up right before my eyes."

Belinda lifted the second sheet of paper, examining it. "Just right there on the pad?"

"Yes."

"Like, burned, burned?"

"Yes. Flames just marched right across the page with the pad sitting on my desk. I tried to put it out. That's how the second page got all smeared."

"This page looks fine," she said, looking over the pad at him.

"I know. That's the kicker."

She put the pad on the nightstand and slid to the edge of the bed. "That doesn't make any sense, Sweetie." She extended her arms to him. "Are you sure something didn't start it? A candle, or maybe a cigarette?"

"I told you I'm not smoking again, and I hate candles. You know that. There was nothing in the room to light it. It just started on its own."

"Are you sure you didn't dream it?"

Carver ran his finger along the charred edge of the paper and held it before her. "Does this look like a dream?" he asked, showing her the blackened tip of his finger.

Belinda bit her lip as she looked from Carver to the pad, then back to Carver. "It just…"

Carver nodded emphatically. "Poof," he said, making two fists and then splaying his fingers suddenly.

"And you're sure…"

"I'm sure." He came to her and kneeled, allowing her to embrace him. "It's the damnedest thing I've ever seen." He looked at the pad as his arms wrapped around her waist. "What do you think it means?"

"I don't know, Babe. Did the smoke alarm go off?"

"Nope."

"That's weird."

"Tell me about it," Carver said.

"I'd sure like to know what it was that you wrote down."

Carver thought for a moment, then shook his head. "You and me both."

————

Despite the lack of sleep, Carver Willis was in a good mood. The energy and excitement caused by the unusual flame-up spread quickly to Belinda, and with little else to do about it, that energy manifested into a bout of morning sex.

Even the drive into town had been pleasantly congestion-free, allowing him to open the throttle on the Mercedes. The sun was up, it was a beautiful spring morning, and his car hummed beneath him. The smile widened on his face.

As he approached a late model car from behind, he noticed that the trunk lock had been knocked out, leaving a hole ringed in rust. His eyes darted to the road ahead of him, finding it clear. His foot sank on the accelerator. His car responded immediately, and he drew alongside the car.

Carver spared a look at the driver. He was an older black man with gray just touching the hair at his temples. Both hands were gripping the steering wheel. He offered Carver a glance, then turned back to the road.

On the radio, Brian Sandel's monotoned voice droned on about the stock market being up. "Everywhere you look, things are up. The S&P is up. The Dow is up. The index is up. Green. Green. Green. What a way to start the day."

Carver's brow creased deeply, drawn to the announcer's words. He looked down at the radio, then back at the driver of the car he was passing. He gasped, finding a white man with a square jaw staring back at him. His hair was combed straight back, and he wore a cocky grin and a charcoal suit.

"What the…" Carver mumbled, watching the man turn back to the road.

Following suit, Carver turned back to the road just as a horn blared. His breath caught in his throat when he saw the fully loaded log truck rounding a curve ahead of him. He'd have time to get around the guy if he hurried. His foot stomped on the gas pedal, and the Mercedes leaped forward, but did not clear the car next to him.

Carver spared the driver a glance. The man was staring back at him, nodding incessantly. His grin was abnormally wide. His teeth were perfect, like two rows of white Chicklets. The old car's engine was screaming beneath the strain to keep pace with his Mercedes.

"What are you doing?" Carver screamed, throwing a hand up at the driver. He pushed the accelerator to the floor. Now just two hundred yards away and closing fast, the truck blared its horn. The car beside Carver kept pace. The driver kept his eyes on Carver, never looking at the road or the truck barreling toward them.

With the truck drawing closer by the second, Carver knew he had a decision to make. Hit the brakes and drop in behind the man, or press his luck. His knuckles turned white on the steering wheel. His breath came in quick pants.

He looked at the man, grinning like a madman, then at the truck. The truck driver's hand was raised, yanking on the horn. The driver next to him was not giving up.

Carver was about to hit the brakes when the Impala's engine let go in a cloud of smoke. The car faded quickly. Carver snatched the wheel, slipping into the right lane just as the truck rattled past, inches from him. The wind rocked his car violently. The truck's horn filled the car, drowning out Brian Sandel's calm voice.

Rattled, Carver slowed, driving with one hand while the other clutched his chest. "Freaking maniac." He wiped sweat from his brow and glanced in the rearview mirror. An old black man got out of the car and opened the hood. Black smoke boiled skyward from the broken engine.

"Holy shit," he said, shaking his head. He pressed the gas, and the car surged forward, toward town.

# CHAPTER TWELVE

By the time Carver entered the long, sweeping curve that would deposit him into downtown Souls Harbor, his heart rate had settled some, but his mind hadn't. Sure that he'd seen a different driver, he'd spent the rest of his commute trying to reconcile the difference. It wasn't possible, but he was sure that it had happened.

Coupled with the morning's events, he was genuinely spooked. Belinda had seen the charred remains of the page, so he knew he hadn't imagined that.

Starting down the gentle slope into town, he watched the signal light turn from red to green. Working on repetition more than conscious effort, his Mercedes slowed along with the other traffic. He passed beneath the green light in a pack of cars, all eager to get where they were going.

The face of the man driving the old car was locked in his mind. The guy was dressed in a nice suit but was driving an old clunker. And that grin, like he was having the time of his life. It was as if he *wanted* to cause a wreck. But why? A head-on collision with a log truck would have killed him instantly. Why would the guy want him dead? It didn't make sense.

As cars fanned out, Carver stayed in the middle lane. His eyes darted to the vehicles around him, checking the drivers with a suspicious eye. There was a blonde woman applying mascara, a heavy-set man drinking from a coffee mug he'd brought from home, and a young man nodding his head to the music blaring from his speakers. There was no man in a gray suit.

Carver's eyes darted beyond the car in front of him. The traffic light was green. His eyes narrowed as he stared at it. The circular green light stared back at him like the eye of a cyclops. His brow furrowed deeply, and his foot lifted from the accelerator. Was there something about the light? The shape of it?

He glanced at the cross traffic as he slid through the intersection, finding nothing but impatient drivers waiting their turn. Traffic in both directions was heavier than usual. A look at the clock in the dash told him that it was around his usual time to pass through town. Traffic shouldn't be this heavy for another hour.

A flash of color that wasn't typically present caught his eye. An orange, diamond-shaped sign warned of utility work on 14th Street. Carver nodded; that would explain the traffic congestion. He decided to stay in the middle lane to avoid any delays caused by people wanting to make the turn onto 14th.

Brake lights in front of him brought his attention back to the road. A white SUV was slowing. He checked his mirror and switched to the right lane. Ahead, he saw the signal light. It was green.

Carver inhaled sharply, seeing the two previous lights in his mind in rapid succession. The first one was green, and so was the second. And now the third. Green. Green. Green. A memory blossomed in his mind. That's what he'd written on the pad! But there was something else. What was it?

———

Bennie swallowed hard, his eyes darting between the traffic light ahead of him and his passenger side mirror. The light was still red. In his mirror, the strange man was still staring at him.

He stood with his hard hat held to his hip by his wrist and took a long pull from the cigarette in his mouth. Behind him, his coworkers went about their business as if he weren't there.

The ember glowed red between the thumb and index finger that grasped it. The hand lowered the cigarette. Lips puckered tightly, forming wrinkles along them. His eyes squinted. Smoke departed his mouth in a tight plume.

Inside the car, Bennie could no longer hear the surrounding traffic. The only sounds were his heavy breaths, the thunder of his heart, and the sound of the worker's exhale. It filled the car like a gust of wind.

Unable to look away, Bennie watched the smoke race toward him. In his mind, he knew it wasn't possible. The man was fifteen feet away. There was no way the plume of smoke could stay together so far, but it was.

His eyes darted to the light. Still red. He looked back at the man just in time to watch the smoke billow against his passenger-side window. The smoke rolled outward but didn't dissipate. Instead, it continued to roil against the glass, holding its shape like a cloud in a thunderstorm.

In the center, the varying shades of gray were rolling in thick waves against each other. Bennie leaned closer, examining the cloud. A shape began to form within the smoke. Slowly, the colors melded, coming together to form a face. The features were gentle but definite. The eyes were closed.

Bennie leaned closer. "What the hell?" he mumbled. "That's the craziest thing I ever—" He jumped back with a gasp as the eyes opened suddenly. The face leaned in, penetrating the window. The eyes locked on Bennie's. When the mouth opened, it said only one word.

"Go!"

Bennie's foot found the accelerator, and the car leaped forward. Somewhere in the back of his mind, he wondered if the light was still red, but it didn't matter. He couldn't stay where he was for another second. He'd never been so sure of anything in his whole life.

The squeal of tires pulled his attention over his left shoulder. The silver emblem on the hood of a black Mercedes was coming right at him. The memory of his song erupted in his mind as his eyes found the driver of the oncoming car.

The middle-aged man in a suit was fighting the wheel,

trying to prevent a skid, but his eyes were locked on Bennie's.

———

Movement snatched Carver from his thoughts. He tore his eyes from the light just in time to see a car dart from the light on 14th Street. Silver. His foot stomped the brake pedal. Tires squealed, and the world slowed to a crawl.

The Mercedes skidded, its rear end just catching the front bumper of the young music lover's car. The driver panicked and snatched the steering wheel, sending him onto the sidewalk and into a threesome of pedestrians.

The first one of the trio to make contact with the front of the car was a short brunette in a black skirt and a plumb-colored silk blouse. Her upper body slammed into the hood, and her legs whipped upward. One shoe, black with a sensible heel, sailed over the back of the car and into traffic. The man with her had an instant to turn, but that was it. He landed on the hood, his body striking the upper half of the woman, now on her way to a somersault.

Their companion, a tall, thin man in a black suit and blue tie, tried to dive for cover, only to meet the front grill of the car. His face slammed into the headlight, crumpling the wire-rimmed glasses he wore.

The car pushed him through a line of low shrubbery and came to a stop in an empty parking lot behind a consignment shop. The driver sat slumped at the wheel, the cartilage in his nose driven into his brain by the cover of his malfunctioning airbag as it deployed from the steering wheel.

On the street, the sound of screeching tires echoed off the buildings, creating a concert of disaster. Then came the crunch of metal. Beside Carver, a white SUV skidded to a halt in the intersection, narrowly avoiding a collision with the silver Camry. Unfortunately, the driver behind it didn't react as quickly. The red Chevrolet smashed into the back of the SUV, crumpling beneath it. The force of the impact drove the engine into the passenger compartment, pushing the steering wheel into the chest of the young woman driving.

Pinned against the driver's seat by the steering wheel, Helena Anderson sucked in a labored breath and exhaled a slow, gurgling mess. Her left shoulder was broken and useless, but her right hand snaked beneath the steering wheel and wrapped around her swollen abdomen. Her fingers patted it gently, then slipped away.

———

Carver leaped from his car as soon as it stopped, oblivious to the mayhem around him. His eyes were locked on Bennie. He'd run the light and wanted to get out in front of any possible lawsuits.

With each step, his shock and anger faded. Did he know the guy? He was younger by at least fifteen years, with sandy brown hair that hung to his collar. Still, Carver's mind clung to the sense of familiarity, as if he *should* recognize him.

The younger man climbed from his vehicle, leaving the door open. He glanced at Carver, then at the Mercedes. His eyes suddenly grew wide, as if he'd just remembered something important, and he turned back on the way he'd come. After a moment, he turned to Carver.

"What just happened?"

Carver offered his palms. I almost t-boned your stupid ass, he thought as he watched Bennie look around. "For starters, we just missed a hell of a crash."

"Not that," Bennie said, shaking his head. "Don't you see it? Tell me you see this."

"See what?" Carver asked, looking around. His mouth fell open slowly as he took in the scene around them. The downtown area, normally bustling, was eerily silent. For as far as he could see, everything had come to a complete and total stop.

"What the..." Turning, he looked at the wreck closest to him. A red car had plowed into the back of the white SUV that had been next to him in traffic five seconds ago. The height difference had subducted the front of the car, wedging it beneath the larger vehicle almost to the windshield. Tendrils of smoke hung in the air, as still as death, above the crumpled wreck.

Standing in the middle of an intersection of a four-lane thoroughfare, his eyes went to each car on the street. He'd avoided what would surely have been a fatal collision but had caused utter chaos behind him.

A thin black woman in a white minivan was frozen, mid-swerve, ten feet back. The front of her vehicle was just making contact with a Black F-150 in the lane next to her. The burly man driving it didn't look happy about having his new truck smashed. His face was locked in an angry shout, one fist raised in the air as he glared at the young woman.

At the edge of the roadway, the twisted body of a woman wearing a silk blouse and a black skirt lay half on the sidewalk. Her limbs were at odd angles, her head turned away from him in an unnatural position. Even if the world hadn't stopped, something told him she would be dead. Carver's stomach dropped, and he was suddenly glad not to have to see her face.

He wasn't so lucky with the man a few feet beyond her. He was lying in the street on his back. The black suit jacket he wore was laying open, revealing a dark blue shirt. He wore no tie, which registered in the back of Carver's mind as odd.

The guy's left arm was tucked beneath his body. His right hand hovered above the roadway as if reaching for help. The blood that had pooled around his head lay still on the pavement.

Ten feet down the lane, a middle-aged man was battling the steering wheel of a gray sedan with one hand and trying not to spill the coffee in the other. His head was turned to the left, toward a black F-150. Carver followed the path of the car to the man lying on the street. He estimated that the car had stopped about a second before finishing the guy off. He looked away with a grimace, but the scene only got worse.

Further to his left, the parallel lines of skid marks sliced across the sidewalk and through a short hedge. The boxwoods were neatly trimmed and shaped, except for the edges of the gaping hole, through which he could see the back of a car sitting in an empty parking lot.

"What the hell is happening?" Bennie asked, snatching Carver from his macabre tour.

Carver turned back to the younger man and shook his head. "I don't know," he mumbled, barely able to speak. He ran a hand over his hair and shook his head. "I don't know," he said again.

"I know what I see, but at the same time, I can't believe it's real. I must be dreaming."

"Then I'm having the same dream," Carver said, surveying the scene with his mouth hanging open.

Bennie eyed Carver for a long moment, then asked, "Do I know you from somewhere?"

Carver shrugged, his eyes washing over the stilled cross traffic waiting at the light behind Benny's car. An obese man was sitting alone in a late-model pickup. One meaty wrist hung limp over the steering wheel, an elbow stuck out the window. His gaze was locked on the traffic light above them. The man's face wore a look of utter defeat, like he'd rather be doing anything other than going wherever he was going.

Carver closed his eyes tightly. When he opened them, the scene around him hadn't changed. "Shit," he whispered, shaking his head. He turned back to Bennie, finding an expectant look on his face.

"I'm sorry. What?"

"Do I know you from somewhere?"

Carver shrugged. "I don't know. I kinda thought that I've seen you before, but I can't remember where."

Bennie nodded. "Same here."

Carver's hand moved instinctively to the inside breast

pocket of his suit coat, producing a business card. He started to offer it to Bennie, but hesitated. After a moment's thought, he shoved the card into his pants pocket.

"I'm a personal injury lawyer," he said, extending his hand. "Carver Willis."

Bennie snapped his fingers, then pointed at Carver. "Oh, yeah. That's it. I've seen your commercials." Bennie took his hand and shook it. "Benjamin Howard. Bennie. I'm a musician."

"Well," Carver sighed, looking around. "This all looks like one hell of a mess."

Bennie nodded in agreement. "What the hell happened? It's like time just stopped, but missed us. It's like some Twilight Zone shit or something."

Carver's palm rubbed his mouth as he looked around. He didn't want to believe what his eyes were telling him. It was impossible.

Bennie was about to speak when the sound of slow clapping came from the stilled traffic behind them. In the silence, it echoed off the buildings, coming at them from everywhere. After a brief scan of the disaster, both men zeroed in on the source.

Moving to stand together, they both watched a man weave between the cars caught up in the chain reaction behind the black Mercedes. He wore a burgundy shirt beneath an open suit coat and matching charcoal slacks. His dark hair was brushed straight back, revealing a hairline that receded only slightly.

"Well done," the man said, still clapping as he approached them.

"Who the hell are you?" Carver asked, eyeing the man suspiciously. The stranger's shoes wore a high polish. With every step the man took, sunlight glinted off them, sending starbursts into Carver's eyes. He looked vaguely familiar, but lately, that was happening more than he cared to mention.

"Yeah. What happened here?" Bennie threw his hands open at the vehicular carnage around them.

The man paused next to the Chevrolet that had plowed into the back of the SUV. Bending to look in the window, he grimaced and shook his head. Turning with a grunt, he leaned against the wreck and crossed his arms on his chest.

"This is a bad one."

"Dude, what's going on? I mean…look around."

The stranger nodded. "I see it. As a matter of fact, this is the thirty-fourth—or is it the thirty-fifth?—time I've seen it." He shrugged one shoulder. "I've lost count."

"Would you mind filling us in on it then? Because this is some insane shit and it's freaking me the hell out."

Carver took a step closer to the stranger, his eyes wide. "I mean, is this like the rapture or something?"

The man's laughter rolled across them. "Not hardly. He looked at Carver. "Besides, I thought you weren't a believer."

Carver shrugged weakly and looked down at his shoes. "You know what they say. There are no atheists in hell."

The stranger chuckled, nodding in agreement.

"Well, now that that's cleared up," Bennie said sarcastically, "What the hell is going on? It looks like we're the only three people in the world that can still move?"

Carver jerked a thumb at Bennie. "And me and him just narrowly avoided what would probably have been a fatal collision."

The man leaned forward, looking around the SUV at Angie Howard's silver Camry sitting in the intersection. He nodded and looked back at them. "Yep, that would have been a nasty one."

"Look, who the hell are you?"

"You already asked that." The man chuckled. "A lot of times."

"And you haven't answered yet."

The stranger looked from Bennie to Carver, then back to Bennie. He sighed as if he were bored and scratched his right cheek. "I suppose I must go through it all again."

"Again? What in hell are you talking about?" Bennie spared Carver a confused look. He tossed his hands in the air in disbelief before turning back to the stranger. "Why do I get the feeling that you're about to tell us something that doesn't make sense?"

"Because, Benjamin Howard, somewhere deep inside that infinitesimal mind of yours, you know what I'm going to say."

Bennie looked at Carver. "Should I be offended?"

Carver nodded.

"Screw you, dude," Bennie said, stabbing a finger at the stranger.

The man laughed, unoffended.

"Did you cause all this?" Carver asked. Looking back at the man he found him examining the fingernails on his right hand. Inexplicably, Carver wondered if the stranger's nailbeds were dirty.

"No," the stranger replied flatly.

"Then who did?" Carver asked.

"Why, my friend," the man said, pushing off the car. "You two caused it." He spread his hands wide and motioned at the wrecks that filled the street. "You two caused every bit of this terrific catastrophe that currently surrounds us."

Carver rubbed his chin. To be honest, he *had* run the light. Most of the people behind him should have been slowing to stop. He did, however, slam on the brakes in the middle of traffic, but what was he to do? If he'd crashed into the Camry, there would have also been a chain reaction. People would have panicked. They would have probably collected other cars as well. Either way, there would have been collateral damage.

"Really?" the stranger snapped, looking at Carver. "I hardly think that Helena Anderson and her unborn child think of themselves as 'collateral damage'." He man jerked his thumb at the car crumpled beneath the white SUV. "Or Anita Harrison." He pointed to a woman lying a few feet from them, her upper half twisted at an odd angle on the pavement. "Or James Zars." The stranger leaned in and put his open hand alongside his mouth and whispered, "He's the kid in the sporty heap over there." He nodded to the car in the parking lot next to the road, visible through the gaping hole in the hedges.

"What?" Carver asked dumbly. His brow furrowed, and he took a step back. Had the guy read his mind somehow?

The stranger shook his head, raising his hands at his sides. "All these people. People whose lives intersected with yours, even on the minutest of levels, and you never noticed them at all." The man pushed his coat back and put his hands on his hips. He sighed and looked around. "Always in such a hurry."

"I have..." Carver's voice faded as he looked around. The truth was that he had noticed them. He'd seen most of them, but never really noticed them as people, only drivers of cars that were in his way.

"Okay, fine," Carver said with a sigh. "But what does that have to do with all this? I mean..."

The stranger shook his head. "Nothing, really. It's just sad."

"People have somewhere to be, you know. Everyone here is going somewhere. Did they ever notice either of us?" Bennie asked, pushing his chest out defensively.

"Probably not."

"Okay then, let's just concentrate on this mess. What happened?"

The stranger shrugged. A frustrated look gripped his face, pulling one side of his mouth downward. "It's a bad one."

"I think we've established that," Carver said. "Do you know what's going on with everything else? I mean—" he motioned to the stilled cars around them, "—why is everything just frozen like this?"

The man nodded but said nothing.

"Well?" Bennie asked. "If you know something, would

you care to let us in on it?"

"If you want to know what's going on, come with me."

Bennie watched the man turn and walk in the direction he'd come. Turning to Carver, he shrugged. "What do you think? I don't like this guy. He seems like a douche bag."

Carver pursed his lips and sighed through his nose. "I don't either, but there are only three people currently not frozen in place, and neither of us has a clue what in hell happened. Maybe he does."

"Okay then," Bennie drug the hair back from his face. "After you."

# CHAPTER THIRTEEN

Both men followed the stranger back along the main road one full block, giving them a full tour of the catastrophe behind them. At the corner, the man turned right without looking back to see if they were following.

Trailing the man they'd just met, Carver listened to the sound of his own hard-soled shoes on the pavement. He wore them so often that he didn't notice anymore, even in the echoey halls of the courthouse. But now, in the eerie silence, they sounded loud.

Turning the corner onto 13th Street, Carver pulled his eyes from the crumpled bumper of a mid-sized sedan and looked at the man in front of them. He grunted to get Bennie's attention and nodded toward the stranger. Despite walking at a casual pace, his hands shoved into his pockets, he'd put half a block between himself and them.

Bennie nudged Carver with his elbow. "Hey, how smart do you think it is to follow this weird guy to God knows where? If he caused all this, he's probably some kind of witch or something."

Carver looked past Bennie to the traffic frozen on the street. They were passing a red BMW. The blonde woman driving was looking down at her phone.

"Well," Carver sighed, loosening his tie a little. "I don't see that we have many choices." His eyes narrowed as he looked back at the woman. Her mouth was open, and the hand not holding her phone was up in the air, fingers splayed. She looked like she'd just gotten some wonderful news. He turned back to Bennie as they passed the woman. "Honestly, if he did all this, I don't think it matters where we go. Know what I mean? Besides, everyone else in town is frozen in place."

"Do you think it's the whole town?" Bennie asked, shaking his head. "Damn."

Carver looked up, his eyes searching the sky. He stopped suddenly when he found an airplane hanging in the sky. It was a small one, nosed down and headed toward the airport. Behind it, a narrow plume of white hung in a sea of blue.

"I think maybe it's more than just the town." He slapped Bennie on the shoulder with the back of his fingers and pointed to the airplane.

"Holy shit." Bennie shoved the hair from his face, holding it atop his head as he stared at the airplane. His eyes searched the sky for movement but found none. Even the clouds were motionless. "I think we're screwed, man."

Carver nodded as they continued walking. "It's starting to look like you're right."

"This shit is giving me a headache. I feel like I'm in a dream or something. I mean, look at this crap." Bennie motioned to the still cars. "This can't be real."

Carver reached out and nudged Bennie with a fist. "Feel that?"

"Yeah."

"Then I don't think we're in Kansas anymore." His eyes went to a man who'd stopped mid-stride as he got out of his truck. He had on a pair of khakis and a red collared pullover. On the left breast pocket, the words Shirley Consulting were printed in yellow letters. "Well, maybe we are, but everything's screwed."

They walked in silence to the end of the block and crossed the street in front of more cars that were locked in place. Carver looked to his right, where a brunette was reaching into the back seat of a Nissan Sentra. The baby strapped in the car seat reached for something in her hand. Her morning had probably been routine until now.

"Hmm." Carver nodded, thinking about his morning.

It had been anything but routine. Did the burning page have anything to do with all this? Surely it did. How could it not?

He'd written down a list of colors. The three greens represented the green traffic lights. Of course, the silver represented the car he almost crashed into. But what about black? What did it stand for? Nothingness? Death?

"I think we've arrived," Bennie said.

Snatched from his thoughts, Carver watched the stranger open a wrought iron gate and walk through. When they made it to the gate, he paused, struck by the scene before him.

The gate was the only opening in a matching fence that ran between two identical buildings. The larger buildings flanked a shorter one whose footprint was much shorter, leaving room for an elaborate courtyard. Carver's eyes climbed the high walls, washing over the dark red bricks. They were smaller than average bricks, resulting in more mortar joints. The effect gave the impression of red fish scales.

*Or the belly of a snake.*

Two rows of arched windows marked the second and third floors of the buildings on each side. A single piece of pale stone lined the sides of each window, meeting at a prominent capstone. The buildings had a gothic feel to them, leaving Carver to wonder if this was a catholic church. He knew there were some in town, though he'd never been to one.

His eyes washed down to a tiered fountain standing at the center of the courtyard. Clear streams of water hung from the scalloped edges of the top bowl. The surface of the pool below, held at waist level by a larger concrete bowl, was covered with tiny splashes and waves created by the falling water, all frozen in place when the world stopped.

Carver pinched the bridge of his nose, taking a deep breath to calm himself. The fountain and everything around them looked like a moment in time captured in a photograph, but it wasn't. It was real, and he was living every second of it.

Moving through the gate on a cobblestone pathway, Carver felt the temperature drop. He was greeted by an earthy smell akin to a freshly plowed field. Shielded from the cityscape around them, the air was cool and moist, refreshing.

As a kid, the smell of his father preparing their family garden had always been the first harbinger of spring, telling him the cold, wet winter was over. In an instant, he realized how much he missed that smell.

Entering the garden felt like stepping into an impressionist painting. The garden was a riot of color and texture, but his eyes were drawn to a simple windchime hanging from a Japanese Maple just off the path. The copper pipes, tinged with green patina, stood perfectly still, silent. There was no breeze to move them. The butterfly-shaped sail at the bottom hung from a thin black cord that ran through a hole in the middle of the butterfly's head.

Looking over at Bennie, Carver found him with a wrinkled brow and an exasperated look on his face. He was having as much trouble accepting their surreal surroundings as Carver. The men shared a worried look, then Carver shrugged. "We've come this far."

They moved along a cobblestone pathway to a black patio set situated to the left of the fountain, joining the stranger, who was already sitting.

"Okay, we're here," Carver began, his eyes locked on the stranger's. "I think it's time you gave us some answers."

He offered them a flat smile. "Fair enough."

"Let's start by you telling us who you are?" Bennie said.

"You may call me Leopold."

"Is that your name?" Carver asked.

"It will suffice for this interaction."

"What does that supposed to mean?" Carver asked.

"It means just what I said."

"Shit, man," Bennie complained. "The world's all crazy,

and you won't even tell us your real name. What the hell?"

"Fine, Leopold it is," Carver said with a dismissive wave of his hand. "I'll call you whatever you want. It makes no difference to me. Now, what the hell has happened?" What happened and why was more important than the guy's name. He could call himself Rumpelstiltskin for all Carver gave a shit.

"I will tell you, but it's not a short answer."

"I didn't think it would be," Bennie said with a groan. "Why the hell would it be?" he added sarcastically.

The man interlaced his fingers on the table in front of him and began. "I know that you both have at least a rudimentary grasp on the whole space/time continuum process from past interactions, so I—"

"Past interactions?" Carver interrupted, one eyebrow arched questioningly.

"I've never met you before in my life," Bennie added. "I'd definitely remember if I met someone like you."

"You'd think so," Leopold said with a shrug. "But actually, that's not true at all. I'm sure neither of you remembers much." He thought for a second. "Well, maybe snippets, which is odd. Perhaps some subconscious memories do exist. In any event, I can assure you that we have met before. One thousand, eight hundred and seventy-three times, to be exact."

Bennie let out a dry laugh. It echoed off the walls and came back to them sounding hollow and weak. "I'm calling bullshit on that, dude. I've never met you in my life."

Carver looked at Bennie and shook his head. He could deal with this guy. He didn't seem half as tough as some of the insurance agents he'd bested. What he didn't need was Bennie becoming belligerent and fouling everything up. If there was a way to restore things to normal, this guy had to be the key.

"Yeah. I know, right?" Bennie put one hand in his pocket. He leaned in, looking at the man across the table. "Look, man. All we've gotten from you is riddles. Just tell us what's happening.

If you even know."

"That, my good man, is what I'm trying to do." Leopold stood, causing both men to recoil. "Relax, gentlemen. You have nothing to fear from me," Leopold said as he made his way toward a tall stand of orange lilies lining the brick wall on the left side of the courtyard.

"As I was saying, you both have a moderate grasp of the continuum, the fabric of time and space, for lack of a better phrase." He gently stroked the petal of one of the lilies as he talked. "The model of a sun and nine planets rotating around it on a flat plane is complete crap."

"Isn't it eight planets now? Pluto?"

Leopold gave Carver an exasperated look and sighed. "Whatever. Eight or nine, it's still way off base. Space exists in four dimensions, rotating, undulating, spinning as this galaxy and every other galaxy hurtle through an endless nothingness at incomprehensible speeds.

"Most people think that time is linear. As if we're moving through the universe in one straight line, with everything moving in one direction. Lifetimes, generations, are but a blink of the eye. This planet, let alone each person on it, is a pen prick compared to the vastness of space, but it is in that collectiveness that the fabric of everything is created."

He turned back to the men. His left hand rose at waist level, palm up. "But it is so much more expansive than even that."

Bennie and Carver both jumped when a large leather-bound book suddenly appeared in Leopold's hand. Held together with a thick strap, the book looked old and somehow very important. His hand fell slightly as he took on the weight of the book.

Bennie and Carver exchanged another worried look. They were both in over their head already.

"Imagine that the pages of this book are strands, lifetimes." Leopold opened the book and began thumbing through the delicate pages, so thin that the slightest wind might tear them. "There are countless pages moving along countless paths. That's how short a life is in the entirety of everything. Every letter of every word is an individual going about their mundane life." He stopped flipping the pages and looked over the book at them. "Like you two."

He continued flipping, ignoring their mumbled complaints. "People are worrying about finding a babysitter, paying the phone bill, or cheating on their taxes. All inconsequential events in the whole of things, though they seem vital to you now." He stopped and looked up at the men again.

"Each path is affected by every decision made or action taken by every individual on that page." He snapped the book closed and stared at the edge of the pages. "Surely you can see the infinite possibilities that could lead to."

Carver rubbed his eyes, then pushed a hand over his hair. "Okay, so say we can fathom all that—"

"You cannot," Leopold interrupted. "And that's okay. I'm not criticizing you two, but you don't have the mental capacity to begin to fathom how all this works." He held the book up to them. "Most humans are so fixated on their own path, their own line from point A to point B that they hardly ever look up to notice the big picture."

Bennie thought about the blue line on his navigation app and how he followed it blindly, assuming it would get him where he needed to be. "Life isn't always easy, you know."

"I'm quite sure," Leopold said, uninterested.

"I'm guessing you do understand how things work," Bennie said. The man wasn't wrong. He couldn't grasp the concept of limitless realities. None of it made sense to him. The guy had only been talking for a few minutes, and he was already lost.

Leopold smiled. "Yes. I do."

"What does that have to do with us, and all this?" Carver

spread his hands, motioning to the scene around them. "Why is everything frozen?"

"Everyone but us three," Bennie added.

Leopold turned to the flowers, waving a hand over an intricate spider web hanging between two of the stalks. The black and yellow spider in the corner of the web sat motionless, like the rest of the world around it.

"Say this web is everything that exists."

"In the universe?" Carver asked.

A perturbed expression washed over Leopold's face, like a parent trying to teach a child something that they find exceedingly simple. "Everything that ever existed, everything that exists now, and everything that will ever exist. Each timeline is a strand. Finite. Interconnected —" he turned his head to look at the men, arching one eyebrow. "Delicate." His finger rose slowly and gently touched one of the silken threads at the edge. Vibrations moved through the web, radiating from his fingertip.

"Everything that happens here affects what happens everywhere else. That's how the spider knows when something is caught."

"In this scenario, are you the spider?" Bennie asked.

Leopold chuckled. "No. If anything, you could think of me as the gardener."

"Okay, fine. Do we really need to hear all this? I mean, all this abstract stuff aside, how do we fix things here and now? Why has everything just stopped?"

Leopold sighed. He casually tossed the book aside and dusted his hands. The book sailed over his shoulder but disappeared before it hit the ground.

Carver and Bennie shared a look of shock, then turned back to Leopold with wide eyes.

"You two exist on every strand of the spider's web," Leopold continued. "Albeit in different ways and different places. If given time to play out, you'd both eventually die in your own time, as dictated by your decisions, and the decisions of those around you, but the strand continues on."

"So we're not the strand?" Bennie asked, hopelessly confused.

"No," Leopold told him flatly. "You and everyone else that exists are *on* the strand. Moving *with* the strand. I suppose in some existential way you are part of the strand, but you, as one individual, are not the strand.

"Now," Leopold turned back to the web. "Say that one of these strands breaks…" His finger plucked one of the short strands from the edge of the web. "Do you see the reverberations throughout the web? That's what happens. The web survives because of the multitude of strands, but is weaker, if only slightly, because the other strands must now bear the weight of the broken."

"Is that what happened here?" Carver asked. "Did a strand break?"

"No," Leopold said, dusting his hands as he came back to the table.

"That's a good thing, right?" Bennie asked.

Leopold gripped the back of the chair he'd been sitting in and looked at the men. "The strand didn't break on its own. You two stopped it."

"We stopped it?" Bennie asked, shocked. "You talk about all this cosmic bullshit that I can't even understand, and then you say we are the ones who screwed it up? How is that even possible? I mean, we're just regular people, specks, remember?"

"As I've said, each strand is fragile. Delicate. Luckily, most people go about their lives completely unaware of their true position in the universe. There are countless Benjamin Howards and countless Carver Willises just moving through life, flowing along the strand, and behaving normally. They live and they die, and the strand continues."

"But not this one?" Carver asked, scratching the side of his head. "Why this one?"

"That is a good question, and one I've been trying to answer for a very long time."

"I'm guessing you're the one who's in charge of keeping the web together?"

"No. Not even close. I am a gardener, remember? I keep the garden safe so that the web can move and work on its own. The strand is life, it is time, and it is space all at once. It is ever-growing, ever evolving. I can no more control how the web works than a fly trapped in its delicate strands."

Deep wrinkles creased Carver's forehead as he stared at the spider web, lost in thought. "It was the crash, wasn't it?" he finally asked, shaking his head. "The crash was the catalyst?"

Leopold moved his head from side to side, screwing up one side of his mouth. "Not so much the crash itself, but the fact that it didn't happen."

"So it was meant to happen? And somehow, we stopped it, and now everything's frozen in place?"

"Has the strand stopped moving?" Bennie asked.

Leopold put the tip of his left index finger on his nose and pointed at Bennie with the other. "Bingo. Now we're getting somewhere."

"I don't think I like where this is going," Carver mumbled, sparing Bennie a glance.

"It's not for you to like or dislike. Don't you see?" Leopold rubbed his face with both hands. "All the other yous move along their strand. They are all different, all living their respective lives. You both live your lives, and then you die. Some of you are successful, some are not. Some have lived a long time, some don't. Some are nice, some are assholes. But the point is that each and every countless version of you two does not stop the strand. Yet somehow, you two did."

"By not crashing and dying?" Carver asked.

"Yes, but also, by even knowing something was going to

happen." Leopold pulled the chair out and sat back down. He rested his elbows on the table and leaned forward, looking at Carver. "One day, a long time ago, you must have found a way to avoid the crash that took both your lives. Some sort of residue of the event stayed in the recesses of your mind, and you somehow changed the determined outcome."

"Determined?" Carver asked. "By whom?"

"The strand, the people on it, your decisions, your actions. All of it. Each strand is being built as it goes. Each has infinite outcomes. Infinite connections to infinite other strands that conversely affect other strands."

Bennie sighed, rubbing his forehead. "This is giving me a headache."

"You've said that already," Leopold said with a dismissive wave.

"No, I haven't."

"Well, one of you did. Look—" Leopold stood and went back to the web. "I have gone through each and every day of your lives, watched the outcomes and the effects of your lives. I've watched you both be born and die countless times. In every one of those lives," he pointed at the web, "You do not stop the strand. In this one, you did, and it's screwing everything else up." He plucked another strand from the web. "The shockwaves are spreading every time this day resets, and the whole web is growing weaker."

"If there are so many, why does one matter so much?" Bennie smiled, sure that he'd stumbled onto a loophole.

"Because they're all connected by the same energy, the same lives, the same forces. When this one stops, it grates on the others around it that are still moving. This event—or rather the fact that it didn't happen—has consequences on other strands."

"Wait a damned minute." Carver rubbed his chin angrily. "Let me get this straight. We remembered what happened and somehow went back in time and changed it?"

Leopold sighed. "In your here and now, you were supposed to run that red light and crash into him. If that happens, the strand continues. Somehow, you two remembered that it happened and simultaneously prevented it from happening at the same time."

"What the...how is that even possible?" Bennie asked. "Now, granted, I don't understand all this stuff." He shook a hand at the spider web. "But even with this crazy shit you've been telling us," he said, sweeping his hands in a large circle, "that doesn't even make sense."

"If you don't fully comprehend the way the universe works, I guess it would be impossible to understand. The strand is and always was. Every event that happens while the strand is building itself stays on the strand.

"Everything in the past exists as now. If you could move along the strand, you could go back to the now that you think of as yesterday. The now exists as now, and the future will exist as now when it happens. All exist simultaneously, but only the future can be altered."

"Like stair steps," Carver whispered, a vague recollection surfacing from his college days. His Ethics professor was big into quantum physics and used the subject often to pose potential situations to them.

"Exactly. That's a good analogy." Leopold looked at Bennie. "Say that you climbed an infinite staircase. On the thousandth step, the first step still exists, doesn't it?"

"I guess."

"It must, or else the stairway would collapse. Right? You stepped on that step a hundred years ago, but that action still exists. It exists in your memory. It doesn't go away just because it happened in the past. It was built upon. It happened, resulting in you being where you are now."

Bennie threw his hands up. "You know what? I'm done with this mumbo jumbo. I just wanna go home." He looked at Carver and shrugged. "None of this makes sense to me, and this guy is just talking in riddles." He pushed back from the table and stood. "I don't know what you want us to do, but from the sound of things, I don't want any part of it."

"Wait," Carver called as he watched Bennie start down the pathway toward the gate. He turned to Leopold. "Now what?"

Leopold brushed his hand through the air toward Bennie, and he dropped to the cobblestone pathway.

Carver leaped from his chair and went to Bennie's side. As he kneeled beside Bennie's still form, a faint tremor came through the bricks, moving through him like an electrical charge.

A shudder ran through his body, and he looked back at Leopold. The stranger was now sitting at the table, watching him intently. Carver shook his head and turned back to Bennie. After a quick check of the body, he looked back at Leopold in disbelief. "What the hell did you do? He's dead."

# CHAPTER FOURTEEN

Carver stared down at the still body of Benjamin Howard in disbelief. What had been confusion and curiosity about the stranger was quickly turning to fear. It was clear that this man had powers that he couldn't comprehend. A simple wave of his hand had extinguished a human life. What would he do next? Would the guy kill him, too?

His eyes went to the iron gate to the garden. Could he make it to the gate and around the corner before the man waved his hand at him? He wasn't as fleet of foot as he'd once been. Also, the dress shoes he wore weren't exactly made for running. Still, there was a chance if he caught the guy off guard.

*No.*

Carver jumped, Leopold's voice coming to his mind more than through his ears. Turning, he found Leopold standing at Bennie's feet. "What?"

"You couldn't make it," Leopold answered flatly. "It wouldn't matter if you did."

"I wasn't..." Carver stood, giving up on his excuse. "Did you have to kill him?"

Leopold shrugged. "I could have done any number of things, but killing him isn't one of them. He isn't dead. It's the one thing that's forbidden. I cannot take a life."

"He sure looks dead to me."

"Humans," Leopold said with an exasperated sigh as he turned. "Always fixated on death." He took a few steps toward the table and motioned for Carver to follow. When Carver hesitated, he looked back and waved him forward before walking to the center of the garden.

Passing the fountain, Leopold let his fingers drag across

the water in the bowl. The water parted as it normally would, but didn't close behind his fingers. The effect was four trenches on the surface of the pool resembling furrows in a freshly plowed field.

Carver eyed them nervously as he rounded the fountain. Nothing was making sense anymore. The entire world has gone crazy. Clearing the fountain, he approached Leopold, who was sitting on the concrete steps of a small portico at the center of the smaller building.

Behind him, a set of wooden doors filled an arched entryway. The main panel of each door held the intricate carving of a rearing stallion. The knight on its back had been captured mid-charge, wielding a sword above his head. The hand holding the reins also bore a shield that was engraved with a cross. On either side of the cross were the figures of a lion and a lamb.

He stared at the doors for a long time, appreciating the craftsmanship but also wondering about the symbology of the figures. Like most people he knew, he'd been hauled to church on a weekly basis as a child. The faint whisper of a past Sunday school lesson teased his mind but wouldn't come to flower.

Giving up, he tore his eyes from the door to find Leopold staring at him. "Who are you?" Carver asked.

"It's more *what* than *who*."

"Okay, what are you?"

"Simply put, I'm a Keeper."

Carver sighed and joined Leopold on the steps. "A Keeper? What do you keep?"

"This," Leopold said, opening his hands to the garden.

"This place?" Carver asked, confused. "It's nice but…"

Leopold chuckled. "In a way, yes. I do like it here. Given the recent…troubles, it's a nice place to relax. It reminds me of a simpler time." He looked out across the garden and smiled. "I don't suppose you've noticed, but it's quite early in the year for lilies. Roses, too."

Carver shrugged. He'd never been a plant guy, but it made sense. March in Alabama still had cold nights and frosty mornings.

"I suppose it's an unintended consequence of my presence. I've said that I like it here." Leopold sighed. "However, I meant that I keep all of this. The garden, the town, the strand. Everything."

"Are there many of you?"

"Do you mean me personally, or Keepers?"

Carver shrugged. "Both."

Leopold smiled. "There used to be many of me, just like you, but their lifespans have all played out and come to an end."

"That's got to be tough to watch."

Leopold shrugged, slowly rubbing his palms together as he stared into the garden.

"What about Keepers?" Carver asked.

"There are many Keepers. Yes. Some of us keep strands, some keep intangible things like art and music. Some keep love and peace."

"I'll bet those guys are busy lately."

Leopold nodded with a chuckle. "That they are, my friend."

"Did you know he was a musician?" Carver asked, nodding toward Bennie.

Leopold nodded. "I know everything about you both."

"Why didn't that Keeper...I don't know, keep him?"

"It's all about choices, Carver. He'd given up on his music. People are born with gifts. Some see them out, some don't. Your friend there, he was on his way to a job interview when you crashed into him. Or rather, didn't. Thus, our little crisis."

Carver looked across the garden, his eyes landing on Bennie's still form. He'd changed his path, their path, by walking away from music. He sighed, swamped by the enormity of the situation. A complete stranger's decision had changed his life forever.

"He'll be okay," Leopold said quietly. "Trust me."

"Are you going to kill me too?" Carver asked.

"I didn't kill him. I simply removed my protection from him, and he froze like everything else on the strand."

"Protection?"

Leopold drug a hand down his face slowly. "Every time you two don't crash, you freeze, too. Then the whole damned mess resets. But to your question, no. I haven't had to yet."

Carver looked across the garden at Bennie's body. "What about him?"

"Seventeen times." Leopold shrugged. "He struggles with the concept."

"To be honest, I do too."

Leopold shook his head. "No, you don't. Oh, you don't understand everything, but you know enough. You're probably the one who figured it out and put all this into motion."

"What? How?" Carver asked.

Leopold shrugged. "I wish I knew." He interlaced his fingers tightly, bringing them to his forehead. "But now that you know, it makes things more difficult for you both."

"How so?"

"You've already extrapolated what the desired outcome is. You just don't want to accept it."

"The crash is supposed to happen, isn't it?"

"On this strand, yes."

Carver sighed. "That kinda sucks." He thought about Belinda. Outside of a few work friends and his younger brother, she was the only person who'd really care if he died. Her life would be the most profoundly impacted.

He suddenly wished he'd been better toward her. Guilt swamped him as he remembered the countless times he'd rushed her out the door the morning after she'd spent the night with him, all for the sake of his damned precious schedule.

"Regret is a waste of time," Leopold said gently, turning his head to examine a still butterfly on a nearby flower.

"I guess you're right."

Leopold gave him an incredulous smile, then turned back to the butterfly. "She ends up all right, you know."

"Really?" Carver asked.

"Would you rather she not?"

Carver shrugged. "I mean, I'd like to be missed."

Leopold turned to face Carver, his eyes watching him intently. "Would you miss her?"

Carver nodded without hesitation, admitting to himself that he would. "You know, it's funny. Time, I mean. You always think you have more of it than you really do."

"In a sense, you are right." Leopold turned toward Carver. "But that's the thing. There are innumerable versions of you that exist right now. The loss of one doesn't diminish the whole. Your time is greater than you know."

"But the me that's sitting here on this step will cease to exist."

"True. But the others continue."

"What happens if this thing isn't fixed?"

Leopold bent forward, resting his elbows on his knees. He interlaced his fingers and looked down at them. "Connections along the other strands will weaken. Some will break, maybe many. There's no way to tell." Leopold sighed. "To be honest, there's no way to know because this has never happened before."

"I thought you knew everything."

Leopold laughed. "Does a gardener know the exact yield of his plants? He tends them, mitigates the possibilities, and creates the right environment, but in the end, it's up to the plant itself what it produces."

"Honestly, I don't blame the guy for making a break for it." Carver sighed, nodding at Bennie. "Why didn't you just do that thing for the both of us and get it over with?"

"Because it wouldn't change anything. There's something wrong. I cannot erase the past. That too would break the strand. Remember the staircase analogy?"

"Is that why all the weird stuff happened this morning?"

"The burning paper?" Leopold asked with a nod. "I've been ushering you two toward your ultimate demise for a long time. You probably don't remember any of it."

"I think I might. Some of it at least."

"Therein lies the problem." Leopold rubbed his face with one hand and sighed. "This is the part that gets gray." He looked at Carver with a weight in his eyes. "Now that you know, you two have to willingly do this to correct this loop that you're in."

Carver looked down, pinching the bridge of his nose. He took a deep breath and let it out slowly. It was the end scenario that his mind was working toward, but hearing it spoken aloud suddenly made it very real.

"I know that's a difficult thing to ask. I really do."

Carver shrugged and tossed his hands into the air. "What if we don't do it?"

"Then we keep doing this over and over until something breaks." Leopold slid forward on the step. "You two have already crashed and died. There is no moving forward for either of you, no matter how many times you try to change it. I've been moving you both along, slowing you down, speeding you up, in hopes of letting the strand correct itself. So far, that hasn't worked."

Carver thought about the old man in the car he'd tried to pass. In retrospect, all the weird things that happened made sense now. He nodded, clasping his hands together as he stared across the garden at Bennie. The slight charge he felt must have been the strand that Leopold was talking about.

"It was," Leopold said, answering Carver's thought. "It shifted slightly. The strands are constantly shifting, moving. It happens a lot. Most people experience it as an unexplained shudder that runs through them." He looked at Carver and smiled. "Just the fact that you felt it tells me that you're going to do the right thing."

"What about our friend over there?" Carver asked, nodding toward Bennie's lifeless body.

"He may be more of a problem. You see, you both must be in the exact place at the exact time for this to happen. If you speed through that intersection and he's not there, none of this matters."

Carver looked around the garden. "I'm guessing we've been through all this before."

Leopold nodded. "More times than you want to know. It's very tiresome."

"Do I ever run?"

Leopold shook his head. "Not yet. Overall, you've done admirably. Him, not so much." He waved a hand toward Bennie.

Carver's eyes widened as Bennie sat up on the cobblestone path. "So you can—" His words caught in his throat as he turned to find himself alone on the steps. His hands probed the air where Leopold had been, finding nothing. "Shit," he said, pushing himself up from the steps.

He made it to Bennie just as he was staggering to his feet. "Welcome back. How you doing?"

"I don't know," Bennie replied, his brow creased in confusion. "What the hell happened?"

"Man, you were out."

"What?" Bennie looked around, searching the garden for Leopold. "What did that son of a bitch do to me?"

Carver held his hands up. "Calm down. You're okay now. He's gone."

"I was knocked out?" Bennie asked, looking down at his open hands as they patted his torso. "Really?"

Carver nodded. "Cold. I thought you were dead. I even checked your pulse."

Bennie's hand pushed through his hair. "I kinda feel like I

might either puke or crap my pants. What happened while I was out?"

Carver shrugged. "We sat and talked."

"About what? More spiderwebs and cosmic space bullshit?"

"Among other things. Let's get you to a seat. You don't look so good."

# CHAPTER FIFTEEN

Carver looked around the garden. The line of shadow on the wall hadn't moved, yet he felt like a long time had passed. His back was stiff and achy, and he longed to have a scotch on the rocks in front of him. Hell, at this point, he'd settle for a tall glass of sweet tea.

He let his eyes wash over the flowers again, taking his time to really see them. He was no gardener, but he could appreciate the subtle intricacies of the textures and colors, the time invested in the place. Leopold had called them "unintended consequences", but it looked planned to him.

He was beginning to wonder if there was any such thing as coincidence anymore. He wasn't here by chance, and maybe not even by design. He was here because of decisions he'd made, and decisions that everyone around had made. The notion that his life could be affected, effectively ended, by decisions beyond his control felt unfair.

When Benny grunted, drawing his attention back to him, he looked at the man who was a virtual stranger. All he knew was that the guy was a failed musician who struggled with the concept of existentialism.

Bennie raised his head from arms crossed on the table in front of him. "I just don't get it. Are we supposed to just let it happen? I mean, hell, isn't that suicide?"

"That's what I got from the guy. Besides, I don't think it qualifies as suicide. It's more like righting a wrong."

"It's wrong to want to live?" Bennie asked.

"I hear you. I do. Trust me." Carver shook his head. "But I got this feeling that if we don't, then shit's going to get worse."

"What could be worse than dying in a damned car wreck?"

"I don't know. Causing other people to die?" Carver leaned forward. "Think about the crash site. I don't know about you, but I counted at least a half dozen dead people. There may be more."

"Who's to say all that wouldn't happen anyway?"

Carver shrugged, tired of the whole discussion.

"But why us? Why do we have to die? Why can't it be some other form of us on some other damned string, or whatever the hell it's called?"

Carver shrugged. "I don't know, man. But if it was, don't you think they'd ask the same question? Hell, I don't understand it much better than you. All I know is that he says that this was meant to be, and we screwed it up somehow."

*You screwed it up, and then you told him about it.*

Bennie shook his head adamantly. "I got a wife, man. What about her? How does she play into this bullshit scheme? Does she even matter to this guy?" Bennie jerked his thumb to the side as if Leopold were standing beside him. "Does he even care about her?"

"I know what you're talking about. I have someone, too." Carver rubbed his left eye with his fingertips. "He didn't mention anyone else."

"And you're okay with just abandoning her?"

Carver tossed a hand into the air. "Do we have a choice?"

"I say we do."

"Then let me hear it because I ain't got jack squat for ideas."

"Well..." Bennie struggled to finish the sentence. He paused to think and then said, "I mean, we could..."

"See? This guy, Leopold, he's been pushing us to this point so that it happens like it's supposed to."

Bennie thought about the utility worker. In his mind, he saw the face protruding from the smoke as it billowed against his window. He couldn't be sure, but it had a resemblance to Leopold.

"Like how?"

"Any weird stuff happening lately that you can remember?"

"Yeah. Maybe," Bennie lied.

"Well, there's been lots of weird shit happening to me." Carver slid forward in his chair. "Look, this guy just waved his hand, and you dropped like a sack of bricks. I mean, he's got powers that we can't imagine. I seriously doubt if he's going to let this go. I mean, how can he?"

"Still," Bennie persisted, shaking his head as he chewed on a thumbnail, lost in thought.

"I don't know what else to say." Carver leaned back in the chair and threw his arms out at his sides. "Look around, dude. Everything has stopped except for three people. Me, you, and this guy. I don't have any superpowers, so unless you can fly or some shit, I don't think we have a choice. We're just going to keep doing this over and over again."

"He doesn't have superpowers. I think he's full of crap."

"Really? He made a book appear out of thin air. I know you saw that because I saw it plain as day. Oh, and don't forget that he knocked you cold with the wave of his hand. You were gone, man. Out. He's not a bullshitter. I'll be honest. I don't know if he is what he says he is, but he's no bullshitter. He's something."

"Even if he is who or what he says he is, you can't just show up and ask two people to kill themselves. This ain't 'take one for the fucking team', man. It's our lives."

"Don't you think I know that?" Carver snapped, sharper than he intended. "But at some point, we have to face the facts."

"I haven't heard any facts, just a bunch of psychobabble about time and space. This ain't some Star Trek episode, man. Shit." Bennie shook his head. "Spider webs and strands and multi-dimensions. It sounds like a load of shit."

"If it were an episode of Star Trek, I'm afraid we'd be the guys in the red shirts." Carver laughed despite the weight of the situation.

"I'm glad your life is so complete that you don't mind dying."

"Not even close, man," Carver told him. "You think I don't have any regrets?"

"Well, you sound like you've decided to just let yourself be killed. I mean, what if this guy is some kind of witch or something?"

"Really?" Carver asked. "Look around."

"All I'm saying is, why should we believe him?"

"Maybe because he's the only other person in the freaking world not frozen in place."

"Still." Bennie shook his head and started chewing on his thumbnail again. "We don't know it's the whole world anyway."

Carver scoffed. "Don't you get it? We don't have a choice. According to him, it's already happened. We're already dead."

"I'm not dead." Bennie snapped. "And you're starting to sound as full of shit as that nutcase."

"He said we died in the first collision, but something happened, and we screwed up the strand. We caused all of this!"

"How!" Bennie screamed, pounding his fist on the table. "How? Tell me that. How did two regular fucking people screw up the whole damned universe?"

Carver shrank into his chair. It was a good question. How did they? Surely the existence of the universe had a built-in failsafe. It had to have.

"I don't know," Carver finally said with a weak shrug.

"That's what I thought."

Carver watched Bennie stand from the table fast enough to topple his chair, turn, and head for the gate. "Where are you going?"

Bennie threw up a hand. "Away from here."

"You're as guilty of causing this as anyone," Carver called after him.

Bennie stopped and spun on a heel. "What the hell is that supposed to mean?"

"You changed your path by walking away from your music." Carver nodded, absorbing Benny's glare. "He told me all about your job interview. That's why you were in that intersection."

Bennie stabbed a finger at Carver. "Screw you, man. You don't know shit about me."

"You're right. I don't, but he does. He knows you were going to get a job."

"Don't try to pin this shit on me. What about you? Huh? What about the choices you made that landed you here? You ever think about that? Last time I looked, we were in the same fucking boat."

Carver nodded in agreement. "That's true. Look, we both made decisions that led us to this exact point in time, originally at least. We crashed and we died. Both of us. But the world kept going." He rose from the table and spread his hands wide. "Look around, Bennie. Does this look normal? Should this be happening?"

"We didn't make this happen."

"Didn't we?" Carver stared into Bennie's eyes, finding only confusion and fear. "Look, man, I feel just like you do. I don't want this to happen, but it's already done. I don't know how, but we screwed it up. What's that thing they say? Dead man walking? That's what we are. Nothing's going to change that."

"This is bullshit."

"Probably so, but that still doesn't change anything."

"What the hell is wrong with you, man? You act like you've made up your mind and actually *want* to do this."

Carver shook his head. "That's not even close." He threw his hands up and let them fall. "Look around. The freaking world has stopped! It stopped. Frozen in place. Everything and everybody." He waved a hand at the road behind Bennie. "The cars, the people in them." He pointed to the sky. "The planes, clouds. The wind. The spider. It's all stopped. That, in and of itself, should tell you that something's wrong. Bad wrong. And since there's only the two of us, it's up to us to make it right."

"Right?" Bennie asked, stomping back to Carver. "Right? This morning, I had to decide if I wanted to stay with my wife or abandon my dreams. What kind of choice is that to have to make? Is that right? I had to choose to take a crappy stinking construction job just to pay the fucking power bill or pursue the one thing in this whole damned stinking world that I'm good at; that makes me whole, that brings me joy. Tell me, mister hotshot lawyer, what the hell is right about that?"

Carver sighed, searching for the right words. "Not one damned thing. Nothing's right about that. But it happened. Look, there's stuff in my life that I wish I could change, too, but it's too late now. What's done is done. For whatever reason, we both made choices that ended in a collision that killed us both. The only choice we have is if we want to screw it up for everybody else, too."

# CHAPTER SIXTEEN

Belinda opened her eyes, slowly focusing on the figure lying beside her in bed. Though backlit by the nightlight in the bathroom, she could see Carver's smile.

"Good morning," she said, smiling herself. "You're up early."

Carver shrugged one shoulder. His hand found the curve of her hip beneath the covers and caressed it. A gentle moan escaped him. "I've been wanting to do that for a while."

"Why didn't you?" she asked, moving closer to him.

"I didn't want to wake you."

"Aw," she cooed and snuggled closer to him. "You're sweet."

Carver's hand slid up her body, allowing his fingertips to drag along her side and over her shoulder. He brushed a lock of hair behind her ear and caressed her cheek with his thumb. "Do you know how beautiful you are?" he asked quietly.

"Please," she scoffed. "I probably look like death warmed over." She ran a hand through her hair. "But thanks for saying so."

"It's true. I haven't told you that enough."

"Hmm. Is someone feeling frisky?" she asked, an arm snaking around him. Moving closer, she kissed his lips.

"Maybe." Carver shrugged one shoulder. "But later."

"Okay," she said, content to cuddle.

Carver wrapped his arms around her waist and pulled her to him. He'd been awake for hours. After taking care of some business that required waking his secretary, he'd come back to bed and watched Belinda sleep.

Lying in the dark, holding her warm body against him, he

wondered how she'd react when she heard the news.

Somehow — undoubtedly through Leopold's hand — he'd awakened with full memory of today's events. He'd played and replayed the scene from memory, focusing on details that he'd seen but not registered yesterday.

He re-lived the tour he and Bennie had taken after leaving the garden. They'd visited each wrecked vehicle, each fatality. The people didn't seem dead. There was little blood spilled because everything had stopped so abruptly, but their vacant eyes told him that they were gone. It wasn't easy, but he felt he needed to do it to get the full scope of what they'd done.

They were all people who were just going about their morning. How many of them had shopping lists in their pockets? How many had kids at home? Who was in love? Who was lonely?

In the end, the size of the catastrophe was reduced to one woman in one car, the red Chevrolet that had slammed into the back of the white SUV. The woman's head was slumped to the side, her body held against the seat by the steering wheel that had been shoved into her chest. The sun shone through the shattered window, lighting the fine hairs on her slender arm as it lay against her distended abdomen. With her dying breath, she'd tried to comfort a child that would never be born unless they did something.

Bennie had turned away, but he couldn't. He stared at the woman he'd never met, and his mind asked him questions he'd never be able to answer. How far along was she? Was it a boy or a girl? Did she have a name picked out yet? A color for the nursery?

In the end, he began to cry, and the still world around him began to fade. The next thing he knew, he was waking up in his own bed. Another day had begun, and choices had to be made.

"Penny for your thoughts," Belinda whispered.

"Oh, nothing in particular," Carver lied.

"Yeah, right," she laughed, poking him in the ribs. "You're

never thinking about nothing."

Carver wrangled her hand from beneath the covers and kissed it. "Honestly, I was thinking about you and me. Us. I've kinda been a jerk to you."

"Oh," she said, pulling her hand free and using it to tug the covers back over them. "Most guys are jerks sometimes. You ain't so bad."

"Why do you put up with me? You're young and beautiful. You could do better than me."

Belinda smiled. "Look, my first husband was gorgeous. I mean, he was an Adonis. He worked out a lot. His abs were to die for. I mean, a girl could just—"

"Okay. I get the point," Carver said, rolling his eyes. "I'll stipulate to the fact that he was hot."

Belinda chuckled softly as her hand came up and stroked Carver's face. "He was also a completely self-absorbed jerk. I mean, a real natural-born asshole. He always made these comments about my body, kinda backhanded stuff at first, you know. It didn't take long for him to be outright mean about it. He made me feel like shit all the time, even in public." She shook her head and sighed. "You're not perfect, neither am I, but you've always made me feel like I was beautiful. I feel like you want to be with me, even around all your lawyer friends."

Carver pulled her to him and kissed the top of her head. "You are beautiful, and I do want to be with you."

"Thank you." She rose onto an elbow. "You wanna know when I started falling in love with you?"

"After we had sex for the first time?" he asked, wiggling his eyebrows.

"No," she laughed. "We were at that fancy restaurant downtown, the one that shut down a while back."

"Jonah's?"

"Yeah. That's it. We were both dressed up. I so wanted to be one of those thin girls for you that I bought a dress that was too tight. You complimented me on my outfit, but I knew I looked like a busted can of biscuits in it. I saw in your eyes that you meant it too. But the thing that got me was that when we were walking in, you held the door for me and put your hand on the small of my back and walked in next to me."

"That was it?"

She shrugged. "I don't know. Maybe it's silly, but when I was a teenager, I read in a magazine that if a man puts his hand on the small of your back and walks with you, that he cares for you, respects you, and wants everyone to know that you're with him, but he also respects you. That meant a lot after what I'd been through."

"I did. I mean, I do. Maybe I just never realized how much."

She gave a flat smile. "Sometimes our subconscious knows before we do."

"But, if I remember correctly, we did sleep together that night. Surely that cemented things for you."

"Yes," she said, her smile widening. "You rocked my world, and I knew right then that I could never live without you."

"Good to know," Carver laughed. "I'm not a kid anymore. I put a lot of preparation into that night, for your information. I even left work early and took a nap so I wouldn't be tired."

Belinda laughed and rubbed his cheek again. "You're sweet. And it really *was* wonderful."

Carver rolled onto his back with a sigh and pulled her to his chest. "Do you ever wish you could change things?"

"Like what?"

"I don't know. The past. Maybe do things differently. Better."

"No," she said, running her fingers through his thin crop of chest hair. "If things were different—before I mean—then we might not have ever met and we wouldn't be here today. I mean, if my ex hadn't been an ass, I wouldn't have had to go through that, but I also wouldn't be here now."

Carver nodded, his hand finding her shoulder and caressing it. "It hardly seems like a fair trade, if you ask me." In the garden with Leopold, he'd been so sure of his decision to go through with it, to put things right. Now, however, he was wavering.

This was nice, this vulnerability that he and Belinda were sharing. He suddenly wanted more time to enjoy it and her. Life in general. He'd worked tirelessly to get to this point and had missed out on a lot.

He suddenly wanted to take Belinda to Paris, Bora Bora, Hawaii. He wanted to make her happy and cherish her laugh more. He wanted to lie in bed, their naked bodies entwined, and watch a thunderstorm roll through.

"You've made me happy, Carver. Thank you."

He squeezed her. "You've made me happy, too. Sorry if I didn't tell you enough."

"You don't have to say it, but thanks." Belinda sighed, and her hand stopped on his chest. She laid her palm against his flesh for a moment. "Why is your heart racing?"

"It's just you."

"Yeah, right."

"It is. Really." His hand left her shoulder and slid down her body to her butt, giving it a squeeze. "See?"

"Um-hum. What's on your mind? And don't say work because I know it's not."

"To be honest, I can't tell you. Or at least I don't think I can. Or maybe I shouldn't. I don't know. But I've been thinking about something." He used his free hand to rub his face. "What if you could do something, something big, that would help out a lot of people, but it would also hurt a few people close to you?"

"Hurt how?"

"Make them sad, I guess. For a while."

"Hmm. How bad would the whole lot of people be affected

if you didn't do it?"

"Pretty bad, I'd guess." He nodded, thinking about the faces he'd seen frozen in place. "Yeah. Bad."

Belinda sighed, thinking. After a moment, she resumed rubbing his chest. "You know me, I always say that people should think about the whole before the individual. Remember, you called me a socialist that one time."

Carver laughed. "True, but it's not always that easy," he said, remembering Bennie's reaction. "Sometimes it's hard as hell."

"I'm sure it isn't easy. But is it the right thing to do?"

Carver nodded. "Probably so. I mean, yeah."

"Then do what's right, sweetie."

"I don't want to. I mean, I thought I did, but now I don't."

"What's changed?"

Carver sighed as he pushed a hand through his hair, leaving it resting on the top of his head. "Everything."

# CHAPTER SEVENTEEN

Bennie folded the three-page letter in half and wrote Angie's name on the outside. Standing it like a tee pee over the saltshaker on their kitchen table, he sighed and stared at it for a moment. This was his last chance to back out.

He sat in silence, weighing his decision. He didn't want to leave Angie like this, but there wasn't any other way. If he stayed, he'd get maneuvered into a crash and die. She was going to lose him either way. Maybe this way, he could change things.

Standing, he crossed the room, grabbing his guitar on the way to the door. He couldn't do it. He wouldn't. He deserved his full chance at life, and nobody was going to take it from him. Not some hot-shot lawyer and definitely not some nutjob spouting off about threads and spiders and shit. No way.

He stepped into the predawn cool of the porch and quietly closed the door behind him. In the letter, he'd explained that Angie could find her car at the bus station and that he was going to L.A. He was either going to make it or die trying. When he'd made enough to support them, he'd send for her. If she didn't hear from him, she'd know that she married a failure. She should count her blessings that he'd left. At the very least, there'd be fewer Raman noodles to buy.

In his letter, he told her not to try to change his mind. He loved her, but he had to do this. He had to know if he could do it. He'd opened his heart to her, shedding tears of pain and fear in the process.

What he didn't tell her was that he was trying to escape an early demise, that he was hoping to alter the trajectory of everyone's life. He didn't say that if he wasn't at the intersection of 14th Street and Main Avenue at roughly seven thirty-seven this morning, everything might stop. The thread, or chord, or whatever the hell that weirdo had called it, would have to get along without his contribution.

After all, Leopold had said that every decision they made changed the path. He was making this decision. That would change everything. It was all about the decisions. Why did he have to decide to let himself die? After all, why should he pay such a price just so everyone else could get a shot at having the life they wanted?

Bennie took a deep breath and let it out slowly, hoping to calm his racing heart. He wondered what Angie would think when she found his letter. She'd probably be pissed at first, but would she be sad or relieved after the initial shock? He closed his eyes, trying to get the image of her tears out of his mind. He'd never been able to stand it when she cried.

When he opened his eyes, he scanned the shadows for what he didn't know. The whole neighborhood was still asleep. Across the street, the Abernathys had left their porch light on again. Several white moths fluttered around the yellow bulb, their wings beating silently in the stillness of the early morning.

Moving forward, he dismounted the steps carefully. The last thing he needed was to slip and break an ankle. He crossed the patchy grass, wet with the morning dew, to Angie's Camry. He'd already loaded a Hefty bag of his clothes, his best amp, and a few personal items in the trunk.

He opened the door and put his guitar on the passenger side floorboard, propping it against the seat, then took another deep breath and looked at the dark windows of the house. Yes, this was a coward's way out. Yes, he was running away. Yes, he'd hurt the woman he loved. All of this was true, but so was the fact that he had to go.

There was no way he was going to let himself get pulled into the bullshit that Leopold was trying to sell them. None of it made sense anyway. How could the life of one person affect so much? It was just plain stupid. He was a nobody. It wasn't like he was the president or anything.

Bennie adjusted the seat, then reached for the rearview mirror. When he moved it, he froze, his eyes locked on the reflection of Leopold sitting in the back seat.

"Good morning, Benjamin. Going somewhere?"

"First of all, it's Bennie, and what's it to you?"

"Oh, it's very important to me, or have you forgotten your appointment with fate?"

"I haven't forgotten shit. I just don't believe you." Bennie started the car and backed out of the driveway.

"I know it's a tight spot to be in, but—"

"A tight spot? What do you know about tight fucking spots?"

Leopold smiled, flashing his perfect white teeth. "I know a lot about tight spots. You're putting me in one right now."

Bennie glanced up in the mirror as he pulled away from the house. "Look, dude, you said our decisions affect the string, or whatever. Right?"

"Very much so," Leopold replied calmly.

"Well, I'm making this decision now."

Leopold shook his head. "It's too late. You do remember that you cannot change the past. Right?"

"This isn't the past. It's the now. This is happening right fucking now. I'm driving. I'm talking to you right freaking now."

Leopold shrugged his shoulder, casually sweeping something off the seat next to him. "It may seem that way, but it's not. This is the past, Benjamin. Your life has already progressed to the point of impact with Carver Willis, at which time it ended."

"Then how am I here now?" Bennie glanced in the mirror. "Tell me that. How the fuck am I still alive and here? Huh?"

"I've explained this to you. The past doesn't cease to exist. Somehow, you two happened upon a distortion, an anomaly, or perhaps even created one. And to make matters worse, you both retained at least partial memories of the event and have been messing things up ever since."

"Bullshit." Bennie slowed at a stop sign but didn't stop. "I'm right here, right now." He glanced in the mirror, slapping his chest. "See?"

In the back seat, Leopold adjusted the lapel of his suit jacket and smoothed his tie. "You know that all of this is pointless."

"Nope."

"It is. You are in the shadow of what has happened, whether you like it or not. Decisions were made and events occurred. You are the embodiment of living in the past." Leopold chuckled at himself.

"I'm glad that you find this whole shit show funny."

"Trust me, Benjamin. I do not find it funny at all."

"I don't either, and I'm not going to let that happen to me. I got a second chance somehow, and I'm taking it."

"What will you do when everything comes grinding to a halt again? Will it make a difference if you're on some highway in Louisiana or at that intersection?"

"Maybe it won't happen this time."

Leopold sighed. "It will."

"How the hell do you know?" Bennie shouted at the mirror.

"Do you think this is the first time you've tried this little escape plan?" Leopold caught Bennie's eyes in the mirror. "Sometimes you don't even make it out of the driveway. Sometimes you do. Either way, the same thing happens. Your fate is inescapable, Benjamin."

Bennie slammed on the brakes, jerking the car to the side of the road. Spinning to face Leopold, he pointed a finger at an empty back seat.

"I'm sorry," Leopold said from the passenger seat, Bennie's guitar across his lap. He began strumming as Bennie turned to face him.

"Look, man, I don't want to die knowing that I didn't give this life a real shot. How hard is that to understand?"

"I understand completely."

"Do you really? I mean, you've got an eternity."

Leopold looked up from the guitar and shook his head, one eyebrow raised. "No one has an eternity, Benjamin. Now even me."

"What? Aren't you magic or something?"

"No. It's nothing like that at all," Leopold said without looking up. "I'm just a Keeper."

"Just a Keeper," Bennie scoffed, mimicking Leopold's voice.

Leopold smiled. "You want to know something?"

"Sure, man. Whatever."

"Once upon a time, I was just a regular man like you. That's the important part. All of us Keepers were just regular men and women at some point. It's important because it gives us insight into how you feel, because we felt it ourselves."

"I doubt that."

Leopold went back to strumming the guitar. "We had to accept this role, and one day we'll have to give it up."

"So you'll die someday?"

Leopold nodded as he continued strumming. "Oh, I've been around for a long time. I've watched your grandparents' births, your parents', and even yours. And, I will be here for a long time yet, but not forever."

"You'll get longer than I do."

"I've probably only got a hundred years or so left."

"Well, hoo-fucking-ray for you," Bennie grunted.

"Not necessarily. You see, this isn't always the best gig. I've walked with just about everyone on this strand that is alive now, and a great many who aren't. This is personal for me. I've sat beside everyone who has died on my watch, so to speak. It hasn't always been easy, but I figured I owed them that much."

He drug his thumb across the guitar strings, filling the car with music. Looking up at Bennie, he grabbed the neck of the guitar with his fingers, silencing the sound abruptly. "All life has a beginning and an end. From a house fly that lives just a day to the giant redwoods that live hundreds of years."

"Nothing personal. But that's not a lot of comfort."

"It'll be okay. Really. You've died thousands of times in lots of different places and times."

"Again, not very comforting."

Leopold chuckled. "You think this is bad? On a different strand, you get crushed by this big hulking beam." He slammed his fist into his open palm. "A freak accident. Man, that was tough to watch."

"Is that supposed to be helpful? Because it's not. Not even a little bit."

Leopold shrugged. "But you know, death is inevitable."

Bennie put the end of his fist to his mouth as he stared out the window. "I know death is freaking inevitable. I'm not a child. I'm not even as dumb as you think I am." Bennie shook his head. "I just thought it would come a lot later."

"It comes when it comes, Benjamin."

"How the hell are you always so calm? Don't you have feelings at all?"

Strumming the guitar again, Leopold nodded. "Very much so. I've been through more pain than if you lived a thousand lifetimes, Benjamin."

Bennie rubbed his forehead. "Are there any of these timelines where I turn out to be something?"

"Something?"

"You know, a successful musician."

Leopold nodded. "Oh yeah. Lots of them. On some, you're a big star. Some, a behind-the-scenes guy but still very respected and financially successful."

"That's nice to know."

"In most of them, you have a long and satisfying life."

"What about Ang?"

"She's with you in almost all of them. There are a few where you get mixed up with some bad people. Drugs and alcohol." Leopold looked up, a grimace on his face. "You can guess how those go."

Bennie shrugged, not surprised. He'd known a lot of great guys who went down that path, not to mention all the famous ones who died young because they went down the wrong road.

Looking out the window, Bennie sighed. His breath fogged a small patch of glass, then faded. "It just really sucks, you know. I—and I mean the me that's sitting right here right now—don't want to die."

"Very few people are truly ready to face the end, Benjamin. That's why it's better that people don't know."

"What about you? Didn't you say that you won't live forever?"

"No. I will not."

"How do you think you'll face it when the time comes? I'll bet you're not this calm when it's your time to step off."

Leopold smiled, scratching the back of his head. "We're built a little differently, us Keepers. By the time our days run out, we've been here a very long time. By then, we've seen too much pain, watched too much suffering. In the end, most of us just go in our sleep. It's a very taxing position to be in. It can be very difficult to witness all the cruelty and death in the world, to watch the innocent suffer and die."

"So why do it?" Bennie asked.

Leopold sighed, thinking. "Do you remember the moment you knew you were born to play music?"

"Oh yeah," Bennie said with a smile. He was fourteen and finally got Eddie VanHalen's "Eruption" down on the guitar. It had taken all summer and wasn't in the same ballpark as the original, but people could tell what it was. The sense of satisfaction was so great, so euphoric, that he knew he was born to play guitar.

"That's basically me, but with this." Leopold shrugged and began strumming the guitar softly. "Don't get me wrong. It's not all bad. There is also great joy and happiness in the world. That makes it worth it, I guess. Kinda evens things out."

Bennie nodded. He'd lived through enough of both to know what Leopold was talking about. Once, as a teenager, he'd been asked if, given the chance to know when and where he'd die, would he want that knowledge. At the time, he'd said yes. Now he wished for anything but.

"This just sucks," Bennie said.

Leopold started strumming the guitar again. "Yes, it does."

———

Angie Howard staggered into the living room on unsteady legs. She was stifling a yawn when her heart stopped in her chest. Bennie was slumped on the couch, his chin resting on his chest. In the dim light coming from the kitchen, his skin looked pale and lifeless.

Oh god no, she thought, a hand going to her mouth.

The secret fears that she'd been fending off for months resurfaced. Just some of the things he said, off-hand comments, made her wonder if he was suicidal. He'd taken the band's breakup hard. Like a gut punch, it had knocked all the wind out of him, and he still hadn't recovered.

Standing with a pink flannel robe cinched about her waist, she stared at her husband and regretted every complaint she'd made about his lack of gainful employment. What was more important, money or his mental state? Yes, they had bills to pay, and they had to eat, but what was all that worth now?

The thought of paying for a funeral hit her like a slap in the face, and she gasped. How could she do it? They were barely getting by now. A commercial on TV said it could cost up to twelve grand. Twelve grand. Where in the hell would she get twelve grand?

She closed her eyes, sending tears down her cheeks. Damn you, she thought, admonishing herself. What kind of woman thinks about money at a time like this?

Her paralysis broke suddenly, and she went to him. "Oh Bennie," she whispered.

Bennie woke with a snort, wiping saliva from the corner of his mouth. "What?" he asked, looking around. "What's wrong?"

"Damned you," she said, standing. "I thought you were dead."

"What?" Bennie threw his hands up. "Why would you think that? I just fell asleep."

"Why weren't you in bed?" she asked, falling to the couch next to him. "Jerk. You scared the hell out of me."

"Are you mad that I'm not dead now?" he asked, laughing.

"No. You just scared me, is all." Angie shook her head and pushed a hand through her hair. "I haven't even had coffee, and I get a scare like that. Shit, Bennie."

"I couldn't sleep, so I just came out here so I wouldn't bother you."

Angie took his hand in hers and sighed. "Are you okay?"

"I'm alive, if that's what you're asking."

"I don't know," she said, swirling her fingertip on the back of his hand. "I thought you'd killed yourself."

Bennie grunted laughter. "Not hardly."

"I know that now, but for a minute I thought you had." She sandwiched his hand between hers. "I know it's been hard on you lately, and I haven't made it any easier."

"Stop," he sighed, brushing hair back from her face. "You're right. We do have bills to pay, and it's more than you should have to bear on your own."

"I know, but music is your life, Bennie."

"I do love playing, I can't deny that. But I also love you too." He thought about the tears he'd shed while writing the letter to her. He'd bared his soul with the expectation of never seeing her again. Of course, all that was before his visit from Leopold.

"Maybe when we get caught up a little, you can start playing some local gigs. Who knows, by the fall, you could get some weekend work. I'll go with you, and we'll sleep in the car to save money and eat alfresco."

Bennie smiled, extending his arms to her. When she fell against his chest, he wrapped her in a tight embrace. "That would be great."

"You know that I do believe in you, right?"

"I know you do."

"I guess I just get caught up in these damned bills and it grates on me, you know. I just get so stressed out…"

"I'm sure you do. Who wouldn't? I'm sorry for putting all that on you. I should have been a better husband."

"You stop that. You've been a great husband. You were a musician when I met you. I knew what I was getting into. You were meant to play guitar. I see it in your eyes every time you put your hands on it. It's like the guitar is an extension of your body. You're good, Bennie. You really are."

Bennie kissed the top of her head. "That's all I need to know, baby."

"I'm serious. I'm going to be better. We can work on songs like we used to. Maybe I'll have a few beers and even get up on stage with you every now and then."

"I'd love that." Bennie took a deep breath to steady his emotions. None of the things they were talking about would ever happen, but knowing that Angie was willing to do them was enough.

She pushed up from his chest and looked at him. A hand went to his cheek. "Whatever we go through, as long as we stay together, we'll be fine. We can get through this."

Bennie smiled. "I know."

Angie's smile faded, and her brow furrowed. "Is something

wrong?"

Bennie shook his head. "No more than usual."

"Are you sure? You seem upset."

Bennie shrugged. "It's nothing. Really. Guess I'm just tired, you know."

"Are you nervous about today?" she asked. "I'm sure you'll get the job. Daddy says they're always looking for good men."

Bennie smiled. She had no idea. Despite his talk with Leopold this morning, he still wasn't sure he could go through with it. "I guess that's it."

She searched his eyes for a moment longer, then laid back against his chest. "At least you haven't done like freaking Berg. Have you talked to him lately?"

"I called him a few days ago, but he didn't answer. Why?"

"I was texting with Cindy last night. He took off."

"What do you mean?"

"He just freaking left." She raised her head from his chest and looked into his eyes. "And he took even her car."

"Where did he go?" Bennie asked.

"Cindy said she thought he might have gone to Nashville."

"He plays bass. What's he going to do?"

"Cindy thinks he has a lead on catching on with someone. I don't know." Angie sighed and shook her head before lying back down on Bennie's chest. "She's pretty broken up about it."

"I guess so. That sucks," Bennie said weakly, swamped with guilt.

"I'll tell you one thing, Benjamin Howard, if you ever get the notion to run off on me, you'd better hope I don't find you. Because if I do, I'll rip your balls off."

Bennie chuckled nervously. "Noted," was all he could manage. He closed his eyes, thankful for Leopold's intervention and the fact that he'd torn his letter to Angie to shreds. It lay safely tucked inside the neighbor's trash can.

"You got me," he said. "At least for the rest of my life. That's all I can promise you."

# CHAPTER EIGHTEEN

"Look at us," Belinda said, trailing Carver as he exited the house and stepped into the garage. "We're like an old married couple, me seeing you off to work."

Carver put his briefcase in the car and turned back to her. Her blonde hair was still wet from their shower, and the dress shirt he'd worn yesterday hung loosely on her body.

He paused, his head cocked to one side, and stared at her. It was the first time she'd ever worn one of his shirts, and it gave him a new perspective. He'd always considered her "thick," but his shirt wasn't tight on her at all. Either he was wrong, or he himself was bigger than he thought.

"Is this okay?" she asked, tugging at the row of buttons on the shirt, the top half of which were undone. "I just threw it on after the shower."

Carver nodded, and a smile slipped across his face. Her supple thighs, tanned though it was only early spring, grew from the bottom of the shirt. He'd always thought her sexy, but craved her now despite the rousing session of morning sex.

"Yeah," he said with a nod. "It looks good on you."

Though he truly had feelings for her, he knew they were being amplified by the truth he'd soon be facing. Soon, commuters would be complaining about the snarl in their usual traffic pattern, seeking alternate routes to work and school. To everyone else, this morning would be an inconvenience, but for Belinda and Bennie's wife, the world would change forever.

Carver took Belinda's hands and looked into her eyes. "Anyway, besides, there are worse things than being an old married couple," he said. He watched Belinda's smile widen and pulled her to him. His hands found her backside, and he grunted.

"Aren't you a frisky one this morning? What's got into you?"

Carver shrugged. "Maybe I just realized what a lucky man I am."

"I'm the lucky one." Belinda planted a kiss on his lips.

When she drew back, Carver tucked a stray lock of hair behind her ear. "I have to go."

"I wish you didn't."

"You and me both, babe," he said. He started to pull away, but stopped. "I love you, Belinda."

"I know." Belinda gave him a quick kiss on the lips. "I've known for a while. And I love you too."

Carver smiled, his chest swelling with emotion. He looked at his watch. "I really do have to go."

"Yeah," she said and pulled away. "Be careful," she added, watching him walk to his car.

Carver slid behind the wheel of his Mercedes and closed the door. When he turned the key, the engine roared to life, sending vibrations through the machine. His hand went to the gear shift, but he hesitated. Rolling down the window, he gave Belinda another long look. "My secretary's name is Jean. Jean Wagner. In case you ever need anything and can't reach me."

Belinda's brow furrowed. "Okay," she said, a curious smile breaking out on her lips.

"Jean Wagner. Don't forget. She handles everything for me."

Belinda took a step toward the car, but it was already moving. She crossed her arms over her chest and watched Carver back out of the garage and down the driveway. He paused to allow a passing car to clear, then backed into the street.

Her brow creased deeper, and she realized that her heart was racing in her chest. A knot formed in her stomach as an ominous feeling fell over her like a blanket.

She hurried out of the garage and down the drive, her

bare feet slapping on the concrete. At the end of the drive, she shielded her eyes from the morning sun and looked for Carver's black Mercedes.

He was pulling off from a stop sign a block away. The sun glinted off the car's back windshield, shooting rays of light at her. The lyrics of a song sprang into her mind as she watched him leave.

*If the truth means losing you, then baby, tell me lies.*

Belinda pursed her lips and shook her head. "Please be careful," she whispered, watching the black Mercedes disappear around a curve.

———

The pneumatic doors closed behind Angie Howard with a whoosh, but she didn't hear it. Stopped just inside the hospital, she was suddenly swamped by the sound of music coming gently from the speakers in the ceiling.

Typically just indecipherable instrumental background noise, she rarely even heard it anymore. But this, this was different. There were lyrics, and she recognized them instantly!

*"If the truth means that it's over…Then please, baby, tell me lies. 'Cause I'm stuck here in a prison… where dreams go to die. I might be losing my mind. I might be going crazy. Or just waiting for death to come…in a big black Mercedes."*

She gasped, her eyes growing wide. Spinning, she hit the metal pad next to the doors. She rushed through the narrow gap as they opened. Her eyes scanned the parking lot, looking for movement. When she found a silver Camry sitting at the stop sign on the far edge of a lot, she raised her hand and took a few steps toward it.

When the car pulled onto the road and sped away, she stopped. As her car disappeared behind a line of tall hedges, a gust of wind swept across the lot, lifting a lock of hair from her face.

A hand went to her mouth as she processed the sense of

foreboding that threatened to swallow her. Her chest grew tight around her thundering heart. Her stomach knotted violently. Something was wrong.

Fishing her cell from the front pocket of her scrubs, she dialed Bennie's number. Her free hand patted her hip repeatedly while the phone rang. Taking a few more steps along the sidewalk, her eyes went back to the street in front of the hospital. "C'mon, Ben, answer the damned phone."

"Hello," came Bennie's voice through her phone, giving her a moment of hope.

"Hey, look, I—"

"Ha! Gotcha. Just leave a message, maybe I'll call," his voice interrupted.

"Shit," Angie snapped. She ended the call and redialed the number. By the time Bennie's voice repeated its message for a second time, she was nearly frantic.

"Hey, girl. You okay?"

Angie looked around to find a young woman dressed in the same color scrubs. She pulled her long, dark braids through her hand and brought them to the front of her right shoulder while her eyes surveyed Angie.

"What? Oh. Yeah, Cindy. Just trying to call Bennie." Angie forced a smile for her coworker, but it did little to alleviate the woman's concerned look.

"Things going okay with you two?"

Angie nodded, dropping her phone back into her pocket. "Yeah. I just wanted to remind Bennie of something." She offered another smile and a dismissive wave.

"You look a little out of sorts. You sure you're okay?"

"Oh yeah. It's all good," Angie lied. "I'll just call him later." What else could she say? That she was suddenly sure that her husband was in danger? That she had a bad feeling about today?

"Okay. Good." Cindy followed Angie as she turned and

headed back into the hospital. "Did you hear what Janice told Doctor Rayburn?"

"Uh. No. I don't think so." Angie spared a look over her shoulder at the stop sign where she'd last seen Bennie. Beside her, Cindy launched into a bout of gossip. As they entered the building, quiet instrumental music sifted down from the speakers. In her heart, something told her that she'd seen her husband for the last time. It didn't make sense, but she was sure of it.

Walking alongside her coworker on unsteady legs, Angie's eyes washed over familiar surroundings that suddenly felt distant, detached. Someone had left a gurney in the hallway. The top sheet was pulled back. There was a small stain on the bottom sheet. From the color, it could have been old blood or fresh poop.

A nurse pushed an elderly man past them in a wheelchair. The nurse's smile faded, and her brow creased when she noticed Angie's worried face. The old man, hunched forward, never looked up.

How could she work today? Her head was spinning. Everything felt out of place. Her breath was coming in hitchy pants, catching in her throat. Her chest felt like it was about to explode. Her stomach hurt.

"Look, Cindy," she said, stopping in the hallway.

"Damn girl, you're as white as a sheet. You sure you're feeling okay?"

"I don't know." Angie leaned against the wall and covered her face with her hands. She took a long breath through them and exhaled slowly. "You ever just get a feeling that something's wrong?"

"I don't guess," Cindy said with a shrug. "Never anything that made me feel like you look." She rubbed Angie's shoulder. "You look like you got morning sickness. You ain't pregnant, are you?"

Angie shook her head. "No. I don't think so anyway."

She dropped her hands and took another deep breath, letting it out slowly. Oh god, she thought. If I am pregnant…the financial ramifications would be a disaster.

Cindy put the back of her hand to Angie's forehead. "No fever, but you're kinda clammy."

"Thanks. It's okay. I feel a little better now." Angie's chest had loosened some. "Maybe it's just a blood sugar thing. Me and Bennie had biscuits and gravy this morning, and I probably had too much coffee."

"Mm-hmm. That'll do it. I usually just keep a two-liter Coke and have a glass over ice. Coffee gives me the jitters."

Angie pushed off the wall, smiling at two doctors as they passed, eyeing her curiously. She ran a hand through her hair and sighed. Her day had started with her thinking she'd found her husband's dead body, moved to thinking that something was wrong, and had just landed on the possibility that she may be pregnant. Her shift hadn't even started yet, and she was already mentally spent.

# CHAPTER NINETEEN

At the stop sign on Highway 11, Carver took a moment to check himself in the mirror. The Windsor knot in the yellow tie lay perfectly against the dark teal shirt he wore. They were a Christmas gift from Belinda. He hadn't worn them yet, citing the fact that they weren't "court appropriate", like his typical white shirt and plain tie. His eyes danced along the silk, dotted with tiny teal fish, admitting that it did look nice.

He smoothed his tie against his chest and tugged at the lapels of his jacket. He'd chosen a soft gray suit to die in. It felt like a dream. He was actually driving to his own death. Willingly. Everything else was normal. The scenery was the same as every other day. The same traffic shared the road, but today would be different.

This was his last commute. Everything he did would be the last. Last time he passed 'the old man'. Last time he stopped at this sign. Last time he hurried to beat a red light.

"How magnanimous of you, old chap," he said to his reflection. "Way to take one for the team." He smiled, but it was forced. Fear hung in his eyes.

When the last car passed, he pulled onto the highway and fell in line. His usual impatience was missing this morning. Things would work themselves out to make sure he'd be in the right place at the right time. Or rather, Leopold would work them out for him. He briefly toyed with the idea of testing Leopold's abilities but dismissed it. Today was no day for games.

Driving in silence, his thoughts turned to Leopold and his explanation of the situation. There was no denying what had happened. Both he and Bennie saw the world standing still—the effect of him slamming on the brakes and not crashing.

He closed his eyes and shook his head, haunted by the vision of the young expectant mother cradling her stomach. He sighed. At least he wouldn't have that vision in his head for much longer.

His brow furrowed as his mind turned to countless strands, each containing its own version of the world, of him, hurtling through space. All separate yet connected somehow. Who made them? Set them in motion? Why was the balance so delicate?

A hand came up and rubbed his forehead. Trying to fathom the enormity of it all gave him a headache. He thought he might have a basic grasp of the whole shebang, but also admitted that he probably didn't. All he had to go on was what he saw and Leopold's explanation. As crazy as it sounded, it was the only one that made sense.

His foot lifted off the accelerator, allowing a car to turn off the road in front of him. The car's brake lights shined as the car waited for him to pass. In his rearview mirror, he watched the confused driver pull back onto the road and resume his trek toward town, now behind him.

*Leopold's working hard to get me to the church on time.*

Carver sighed, his thoughts turning to Bennie's adamant refusal to accept Leopold's explanation. In many ways, Bennie's reaction made more sense than his own. The guy wasn't wrong. Why them? Why did their paths have to cross at such an ill-timed junction? Why was their meeting one of such consequence? Neither of them was anyone special. Just two dudes going about their lives. Completely random guys.

Surely it wasn't just a mathematical conclusion. Carver rubbed his chin, thinking. What if it wasn't random? What if something happened that marked them? What if something had steered their entire lives toward this one precise spot?

He moaned. It was possible, but highly improbable. He'd grown up around here, but had Bennie? He couldn't remember meeting anyone named Bennie, or even Benjamin for that matter.

There was a kid named Ben Holliday in his second-grade class, but that kid was black. It stuck out in his mind because he was the only black kid in the class.

He spent the rest of the easy commute pondering the possibility. There was no way to come to a definitive conclusion. He'd met countless people during his lifetime. Some went well, some did not. And that was not even counting the ones he didn't remember, people that he met in passing.

Nearing the long, sweeping bridge that connected Highway 11 to downtown Souls Harbor, Carver released a heavy sigh. None of that mattered now. Within minutes, he'd plow into the side of Bennie's silver Camry, and it would all be over.

He would be over.

He wiped one sweaty palm on the pant leg of his slacks, then the other. His heart was picking up speed as his car slowed, matching the traffic. From this vantage point, he could see the path he'd take. It was littered with commuters who'd have one hell of a story to tell when they got to work, late, of course.

He swallowed hard, looking around at the other drivers. Coming alongside the old Caprice with the trunk lock knocked out, he met the driver's eyes. The black man driving had to be in his seventies. Gray hair marked his temples. He smiled at Carver and raised one hand from the steering wheel, giving him a thumbs-up.

Carver stared back at him in disbelief until the slowing traffic in front of him pulled his attention away. Thankfully, there were fewer cars in his lane, and he didn't get stuck next to the man. He'd seen the guy countless times before and thought him just a gentile old man, but now there was something about him that felt creepy and weird.

He rolled to a stop four cars from the red light. A black truck idled next to him. Its muffler was unnecessarily loud. Due to the height difference, he couldn't see the driver, but he knew it was "the angry man" who was shaking his fist at another driver when the world stopped.

A sense of injustice swelled in his chest as he stared at the door of the truck. The guy was probably a real jerk, but would survive the day, yet he wouldn't. For all he knew, the guy was a drunk and a wife-beater. Why did he get to live?

Grunting, Carver pulled his eyes from the truck and looked to his left. His anger evaporated when he saw the woman in the red car next to him. She was young and pretty, with hope in her eyes and an easy look on her face as she fiddled with her hair in the mirror.

When she saw Carver looking at her, she offered a pleasant smile and a half wave. Carver waved back. She mouthed the words, "Thank you." Carver turned his eyes forward. His hands gripped the wheel, and he drew in a deep breath.

"Leopold, if you can affect things like I think you can, please let that child have a happy, healthy life. And a long one."

As the light changed, Carver surged forward, taking advantage of "the angry guy's" lack of attention to slice in front of him. He pressed the gas and moved forward.

Ahead of them, the light turned from red to green. Carver used his momentum to change back to the middle lane and pass two more cars, one of them the sporty model that plowed through the hedges after taking out three pedestrians.

When he skirted beneath the second light, he was already doing fifty. If he was going to do this, he was going to do it right.

He worked his way back into the right lane, cutting off another driver and drawing a lengthy horn blast. His eyes went to the light ahead, watching it turn yellow. He looked at the cross traffic on his right. The silver Camry was there, but the driver was looking back at something on the sidewalk.

"What are you doing?" he whispered. His eyes shifted back to the light. The traffic around him was slowing. That was good. It would limit the collateral damage.

His heart was thundering in his ears as he bore down on

the intersection. His eyes darted between the light and the silver Camry. His breath was coming in rapid pants. His hands gripped the wheel tight enough to turn his knuckles white.

Just short of the intersection, he watched the light turn red but didn't slow. His eyes shifted to the silver car, sitting first in line to his right. What was he doing? If he didn't stomp the gas now...

Carver flew through the intersection, watching Bennie as he went. "Dammit," he growled. Turning, he gasped. His foot found the brakes, and he hit them hard, sending the car into a skid. The sound of tires sliding on pavement filled his ears, then the sound of crunching metal as he plowed into the back of a gray minivan.

"Shit!" he complained, fighting his way through the deflating airbag. The air was filled with the smell of chemical powder and anti-freeze.

Carver unlatched his door and pushed it open with his foot. Standing, he dusted a dry powder from his suit jacket. His eyes instinctively went to the van he'd hit. The crash wasn't as bad as the one he'd intended to have, but it was bad enough. The driver was already getting out, and she looked angry.

He looked at his car and his heart sank. The front of the sleek, beautiful machine was a crumpled mess. His head dropped, and he discovered between his feet the Mercedes emblem from the hood. He tossed his hands into the air and let them drop.

Carver turned back to the intersection. Over the top of his car, he saw Bennie still sitting at the light. Both his hands were on the wheel, and he was looking straight ahead.

"What are you, crazy?"

Carver spared a glance at the heavy-set brunette coming toward him. "I'm sorry. It'll all be over—" His voice hung in his throat when the woman stopped suddenly. She'd inspected the back of her van and was halfway through turning back to him. Hair shrouded part of her face, stilled just as she whipped her head around to face him. Her brow was creased, her mouth in a dramatic scowl.

Carver headed for Bennie, cursing himself for not assuming he'd pull a stunt like this. He'd been against it from the beginning. What was it that Leopold said?

*He struggles with the concept.*

Carver cut the corner, crossing the narrow strip of grass and the sidewalk. "What the hell?" he asked, slapping both hands on the hood of Bennie's car. He stomped up to Bennie's open window, ready to give him what for, but the look on the kid's face silenced him.

Bennie sat motionless for a moment, then tossed his hands into the air and let them drop to his lap. His gaze dropped to them as he began picking a fingernail. "I couldn't do it, man. I just couldn't do it. I thought I could, but I couldn't."

Carver's anger faded when Bennie finally turned to face him, paralyzed by the look of desperation and fear in his eyes. In that moment, he saw who Benjamin Howard really was. He was a man, much younger than him, with a lot more life ahead of him. A life that he wanted to live. He wanted to play music, love his wife, and live his life.

Carver's shoulders drooped, and he let out a heavy sigh as he fell against the car. "Shit, man."

"I mean..." Bennie sighed. "I tried to run away this morning, but that guy, Leopold, showed up in my damned car. I ended up going back home and falling asleep on the couch. Angie thought I had killed myself."

"What?" Carver asked, confused.

Bennie shrugged. "Yeah. I tried to leave, but good old Leo showed up. He said that everything would happen the same whether I was here or not. I went back home and waited. Little did I know that I'm too chicken shit to go through with it."

"Well," Carver said, waving a hand at the still cars surrounding the intersection. "Obviously, he was right."

"The thing is, when I was sitting on the couch, I got to wondering why us? Know what I mean? Why you and me? We're not anyone important. How could us two have such a major role to play in all this shit?"

Carver shrugged and shoved his hands in his pockets. "To be honest, I was thinking the same thing on my way in this morning."

"See?" Bennie said, leaning on the door. "I'm pretty damned sure there's nothing that connects us."

"I don't know. Where'd you grow up?" Carver asked.

"South of Montgomery. I only moved up here because Angie wanted to. She's from here."

"I'm from here, too. Well, just outside of town. Across the river." Carver looked around with a sigh, his eyes finally falling to the car next to Bennie. He shook his head and let out a chuckle.

The elderly woman driving was staring at Bennie's car with an angry scowl locked on her face. One boney fist was extended across the passenger seat, flipping him the bird.

"Looks like granny was mad at you."

Bennie followed Carver's gaze and erupted in laughter. "Damn. She's pissed."

"What did you do to her?"

"I don't know. Maybe she knew I'd screw things up."

Carver rubbed his face with both hands as the laughter faded. "Look. I don't know how long we will have before Leo shows up and snaps his fingers, or whatever he does, and we wake up to start this whole shit show over again. Do you remember him talking in the garden about this being the only strand that we die on? At the same time, anyway."

Bennie shrugged. "Not really, but honestly, my head was spinning. I still can't wrap my mind around it, to be honest."

"You might have been out by then, but I'm almost certain he told me that."

"So?"

"So?" Carver pushed off the car and looked at Bennie. "It stands to reason that if this is the only one it happens on, then something about this one is screwed up."

"No argument from me."

"We just have to figure out what it is."

"How do we do that?" Bennie asked.

"I don't know. Did anything happen to you as a kid, something odd, different?"

"Hard to say, really. We moved around a lot. My dad left us when I was a kid, and Mom had a hard time. She moved for work, or when the rent was due."

"Think, man. Shit." Carver slapped the top of Bennie's car. "We probably don't have a lot of time. Did anything life-changing happen? Anything weird or just out of the ordinary?"

Bennie shrugged. "I mean, hell. A lot of shit happened. I can't just pick out one thing." He opened the car door and got out. Bending, he looked at the old woman flipping him the bird and shook his head.

Turning, he found Carver leaning against his car, his elbows resting on the top. His hands were against his forehead, his fingers buried in his hair. Bennie looked at the tailored suit, the cuffs of his teal shirt peeking from the ends of his jacket. His eyes swept down to Carver's polished leather dress shoes. The man had worn a good suit to die in, and he'd chosen jeans and a Soundgarden t-shirt.

"Look, man, judging by the way you flew through that intersection, you were ready to do this thing." Bennie scratched his unshaven cheek. "Now you don't seem so sure."

"Because I'm not," Carver replied. "Leopold said that after the original wreck, I figured something out and told you. Do you remember anything? Some way I might have told you to avoid all this?"

Bennie sighed and shook his head. "I don't remember anything. Besides, I don't think there's a way around it."

"And you'd be exactly right."

Both men turned to find Leopold sitting in the passenger seat of the car driven by the old woman. He looked at the fist in front of him and shook his head. He gently rotated her wrist, then used a fingertip to open her remaining fingers so that she was waving instead of flipping the bird. His work done, he opened the door and slipped out of the car.

He looked at the men and sighed. "I thought we had it right this time," he said. "So close."

"Look, I've been thinking—"

Leopold held up his hand, cutting Carver off mid-sentence. "No. There is no connection. I've been over both of your timelines many, many times. There are one hundred and thirty-seven people that both of you have met thus far in your life. Most are just in passing; the grocery store, post office, and stuff like that. Carver did represent a young man that you know, Bennie, but that was of little consequence. You barely knew the guy, and," he turned to Carver, "You don't even remember him."

"You said that this is the only timeline that we crash into each other. Why is that then?"

"Mathematical possibilities, my friend," Leopold said flatly as he shoved his hands deep into the pockets of his charcoal slacks. "We've been through this before. Two marbles flying around inside a football stadium will eventually crash into each other if given enough time."

"That sounds improbable."

Leopold shrugged. "I didn't write the laws of physics and mathematics, Carver. I, like you two and everyone else in existence, am simply a slave to probabilities."

"If what you've said is true—"

"It is," Leopold said, looking around as if disinterested.

"Don't you find it curious, even a little bit?" Carver asked.

Leopold shrugged and shook his head. "Statistically speaking, there was more of a chance of you two crashing than either of you winning the lottery. But that happens, doesn't it?"

Carver opened his mouth to refute Leopold's claim but closed it without speaking. He thought for a moment, started to speak, but again said nothing.

"What about you, Benjamin? You're unusually quiet."

Bennie looked at Leopold and shrugged. "Could anything I say change anything?"

"Not even a little."

"Well, there you have it." Bennie leaned against Angie's car and crossed his legs at the ankle. His shoulders dropped, and his chin fell to his chest.

"There has to be something," Carver insisted.

"There's not," Leopold said firmly. He rubbed his face with both hands and sighed, calming himself. "Look, on one thread, you die in a helicopter crash. On one, you're shot by a disgruntled client. Ole Bennie here gets squashed by a ten-ton beam. You two, and everyone else, each die in countless ways. This is just one of them."

"In any of them do we die at the same time?"

"No," Leopold conceded.

"See, there you have it."

"See, nothing. It is a happenstance. Different decisions lead to different ends."

Carver shook his head. "It can't be that simple."

"Decision X leads to result Y. Just like high school math class." Tired of talking to Carver, Leopold looked at Bennie. "How about you? You buying into this theory of his?"

Bennie shrugged, never looking up. "I don't know up from down anymore." He pulled one hand from his pocket and pushed the hair back from his face as he looked up. His eyes found a still cloud, and he shook his head. "All I know is that I'm scared and worried, and mostly just sad. I don't want to fucking die, man. That's all I know."

Leopold rolled his neck as he sighed. "Look, I know you

don't. Few people do, but the fact is that you've already died. That's why your thread cannot progress beyond the point you two impact."

"Then why is this happening?" Carver demanded. "Why?"

"Incompletion."

"What?" Carver asked.

"It makes sense," Bennie said. "I mean, I don't want to leave Angie. I love her, man. But the single thing that's been eating me is that my life hasn't ended up where I wanted it to. It feels incomplete. The dude makes perfect sense. About that part at least."

"What about me? I've wanted to be a lawyer since I was a teenager, and that's what I am."

Leopold shook his head. "That's what you wanted to *do*, not what you wanted to *be*."

"That's bull crap."

"Is it?" Leopold asked, looking at him with one brow raised. "Tell me, counselor, are you happy?"

Carver stared at Leopold, his chest rising and falling beneath his suit. What was he asking? Of course, he was happy. He was doing what he loved. He made good money from it. He had a nice house and a nice car. Money in the bank.

"That wasn't the question," Leopold said. "I asked if you were happy."

Carver dropped his gaze to the pavement. He'd thought he was, until today. But things had changed. His time with Belinda this morning showed him what happiness really was. He couldn't remember ever feeling so good.

"That's what I thought," Leopold said quietly.

# CHAPTER TWENTY

Carver Willis woke suddenly. As soon as he opened his eyes, his mind told him that this would be his last wake-up. There will be no more tomorrows. Hell, there would be no more lunches for that matter. This was it. Whatever didn't get done this morning wouldn't get done at all.

He lay still in the darkness, staring at the ceiling. Beside him, Belinda slept peacefully, her gentle snores coming in a relaxed rhythm. He smiled. Of everything he'd amassed in his life, all the stuff he'd surrounded himself with, she was his favorite. She was the only thing he regretted leaving behind.

Rolling over, he looked at the digital clock on his bedside table. The red numbers told him it was 12:07. He had less than eight hours left.

His chest swelled with a mix of emotions. Fear and regret swamped him. His heart began to race. Suddenly, it was hard to breathe.

Closing his eyes, he inhaled through his nose and exhaled through his mouth three times. Regret was a waste of time. That's what Leopold had said, and he was right. He could do nothing to change the past, including the past that awaited him at that intersection.

Opening his eyes again, he felt a little better. The anxiousness and fear weren't gone, but they were manageable. Leopold knew what he was doing when he let them remember everything. Knowing was a nightmare, especially the fact that he couldn't make any major changes to the timeline. He and Bennie had to make the best of what time they had without interfering with the future of those they'd leave behind.

At the same time, remembering every day they'd relived

was almost overwhelming. In his mind, it was like watching one of those flip books where the pages were flipped fast, moving the character little by little. But it wasn't a simple drawing. It was hours and hours of the same morning, all of which ended abruptly at the same intersection.

Carver groaned softly, covering his eyes with the heels of his hand. Given the chance, he'd marry Belinda right now and make her the sole beneficiary of everything he had. She deserved that much at least. Of course, he knew Leopold would never allow it.

With no spouse or kids, everything would end up in a trust to help kids get into law school. That would be his legacy, an obscure endowment that bore his name.

When Belinda mumbled in her sleep, he looked at her and smiled, but his peace faded quickly. Right now, sleeping peacefully, she had no clue what news awaited her in just a few short hours.

Would she collapse when they told her? Would she fall to the floor in tears, crying his name the way they did in the movies? How long would it take her to get over him? A year? Two? Would she visit his grave and bring flowers?

Leopold said she'd meet someone and would end up just fine, but hadn't elaborated. That probably meant she'd find someone else, fall in love, and marry. Maybe even have kids. Eventually, he'd become a distant memory, a ghost of someone she used to know.

His heart sank. Sadness and jealousy consumed him. He didn't want her to have to find someone else. He wanted to be the man to make her happy, but he'd mostly wasted his chance at that. Carver drew in a deep breath to combat the tears welling in his eyes. He said a silent prayer for her to meet a good man and have a good life.

Wiping a tear from the corner of his eye, he slipped from beneath the covers and pulled on a bathrobe before tiptoeing out of the room. He'd wake Belinda soon, but he had a few things to do first.

———

Carver signed the letter and sat back with a sigh. He'd just intended a short note, but when he started, the emotions came pouring out. Five pages later, he'd said everything that needed saying. There was no way to tell if Leopold would allow it, but he had to try. He'd never have enough time to tell Belinda everything he wanted to.

Folding the letter into thirds, he slipped it into an envelope and sealed it. Getting up, he rounded his desk and went to the wall safe. When he raised his hand to enter the combination, he noticed a tremor. He'd spent an hour and a half of his limited time on the letter. Six and a half to go, more or less.

Opening the safe, he pulled out a large bank bag. He grabbed the stacks of money from the safe and shoved all of them into the bag. It was just over twenty-seven thousand dollars. It wasn't a lot, but it wasn't pocket change either.

Screw Leo, he thought. He placed the letter atop the money and zipped the bag. Closing the safe, he turned and headed for the door.

———

The garage had cooled with the night, the concrete floor cold on Carver's bare feet. Not bothering to turn on the overhead light, he fumbled his way to Belinda's car. When he finally found the latch, he opened the door, squinting as the interior light shattered the darkness.

Carver jumped, yelping with surprise when he saw Leopold sitting in the back seat in his usual charcoal suit. "Dammit, man. Do you have to do shit like that?"

"Probably not," Leopold said with a shrug and a thin smile.

"Why are you here?" Carver asked, sliding the bag behind his back.

"I thought you'd have coffee," Leopold said with a wave of his hand.

"Well, I— uh— don't. Actually, I'm just headed back to bed."

"Uh-huh."

"What?" Carver asked.

"Twenty-seven thousand dollars would make a huge difference in someone's life, Carver."

"I bet it would."

"And you agreed not to make any major changes."

"I'm not," Carver lied. "I don't have a clue what you're talking about."

"I suppose that letter and the stack of money behind your back is just..." Leopold shrugged, his hands hovering in the air between them, palms up.

"Look," Carver finally said with a huff. "She's a good woman, and she's not going to get anything from my estate. Nothing. She deserves something."

Leopold maintained his expressionless stare.

"That's bullshit, man. You know it is."

Leopold took a deep breath and let it out slowly. "What happens if you give her that money? Did you ever think of that?"

"I don't know, she takes a vacation, maybe pays some bills while she's getting her life back together."

"She's a smart girl, Carver. We both know that. What if she invests it? Maybe has a run of good luck? She might never meet the person fate has planned for her. Maybe instead, she ends up alone, a rich old spinster feeding her twenty cats gourmet cat food. Is that what you want for her?"

"C'mon, man. You don't know how it will affect things. Maybe it just makes her life a little easier for a while." Carver angrily shoved a hand through his hair. "Shit, man. C'mon."

Leopold shook his head. "I'm sorry."

"Sorry?" Carver asked, flying into a rage. "You're sorry?

What good is that to her? To me? In just a few hours, you expect me to hurtle myself headlong into the side of another car and die. Fucking die! And you want to squabble over a few grand that I want to leave what is probably the only person who really cares about me. Fuck your sorry! How about that? And fuck you too."

Carver slammed the door and spun, intent on going back into the house. He ran into Leopold instead.

"Do you think I have no emotions?"

"To be honest, I don't. It's all about your precious strand and moving things along. You're like that guy at the slaughterhouse who just keeps prodding the cows forward, not caring what awaits them. Keep 'em moving. Feed the machine."

Leopold maintained his expressionless stare, letting Carver finish his rant.

"Just what do you get out of this, huh? You get a fat ass bonus or something?"

Leopold chuckled. He stood in the shadow of the fading interior light of Belind's car and watched Carver's shape move back and forth. Finally, a sad smile crept across his lips.

"I get nothing. I never have." He sighed. "I suppose the only reward is knowing that I may have spared someone some pain by assuring that other people didn't screw up their fate."

Carver grunted. "That's bullshit." He was staring at Leopold when the light faded, leaving them in the dark. "Just who do you think you are? Jesus fucking Christ?"

"I've watched people make critical decisions that led them down paths of misery and pain. I've stood with them at that junction and hoped and prayed for them to make the right decision. Ultimately, though, it's their choice to make. There's nothing I can do about it. I cannot intervene."

"But this time you magically can?" Carver asked.

"It's not magic, Carver. It's the past. I don't understand how, but when you two died, both of you were so full of discontentment that you broke something. Your life was so lacking in the one thing you craved that you couldn't accept the end. Your energies couldn't accept their fates. Shock, disbelief, regret. All of it combined to somehow refuse to disperse back into the universe. That's why I'm here. It's extremely rare that anyone ever sees me at all, much less interacts with me."

Carver sighed and fell against the car. He was arguing over a moot point, and he knew it. Leopold hadn't caused this mess. He and Bennie had. He stood in silence for a long time before speaking. "You know, earlier, when you asked if I was happy?"

"Yes. And you cursed at me."

Carver shrugged. "Sorry about that."

"Don't worry about it. After all these years, I've developed a thick skin."

"Well, I guess the reason I got so mad was because you struck a nerve."

"I know I did. I intended to."

"All my life, I just wanted to be *somebody*, you know. To be something. Now I stand here with just a few hours left, and I have no wife, no kids, no peace. Nothing. As far as I know, the only person who'll even shed a tear is the woman sleeping upstairs."

"Why were you so driven to 'be somebody', as you say?"

Carver shrugged. "My mother grew up dirt poor. She wasn't well-educated. I mean, she was smart as a whip, but just not in a conventional way, you know."

"You mean she didn't have a degree?" Leopold asked.

"No. She didn't, but she was determined for me to have one. She'd always talk about how successful I'd be, what a great man I'd turn out to be." Carver blinked a tear from the corner of his eye, letting it run down his cheek. "You wanna know the pisser?"

"She died before you started making big money."

Carver nodded.

"Do you ever think that money wasn't what she was talking about?"

"We weren't poor, but we weren't rich either. My dad was a miser. There were times when I hated him for not buying me trendy clothes and stuff."

"Kids can be mean, but it's just out of ignorance."

Carver grunted in agreement. "But when I went to college, my old man had saved enough to pay for it. I mean, I had to get a job to pay for stuff I wanted, but my tuition was paid. That's why he was so tight with money all those years. He was saving money for my college. He never said anything, though."

"You were lucky. No debt."

"Yep." Carver shook his head. "But now when I die, I'm just gone. Just like that. It makes you wonder what it was all for."

"No man truly disappears, Carver."

Carver shrugged, tired of splitting hairs. His emotions were too raw, and they were wasting too much of what little time he had left. "What about the letter?" he asked, defeated.

Leopold nodded. "That's fine. You'll be happy to know that it will bring her great comfort."

Carver smiled. "I guess that's something." Reaching out, he found the door handle again and opened the car. Light spilled into the garage, revealing the fact that he was alone again.

"Aaaand now he's gone," Carver said, tossing a hand into the air and letting it drop. He unzipped the bag and removed the letter. He tapped it on his fingertips, wishing that he could leave her more. Finally, he slid it onto the dash and closed the door.

He went back inside, tossing the bag of money onto the kitchen table. As he climbed the stairs, his resentment faded. By the time he made it to the bedroom door, Belinda was coming out of the bathroom.

"You're up," he said, surprised.

"So are you," she said with a smile. "I had to pee. Why are you awake at this ungodly hour?"

"Oh—uh—I thought I heard something," he lied as he went to her. He wrapped his arms around her waist and hugged her tightly. "Didn't see anything. Guess it was the wind."

Belinda pulled from his grasp, leading him back to the bed. "I want to cuddle so close that we melt together."

Carver smiled. "That's the best thing I've heard in a long time."

———

Bennie sat slouched on his couch in the shadows. The dim light from the bulb over the stove crept into the room, glistening on the guitar pick in his fingers. He brought up a knee and hung his arm over it, dangling the pick before his eyes.

How many picks had he gone through? A thousand? Two thousand? How many had Angie found in the washing machine, on the floor?

It was so small, seemingly insignificant to so many people, but vital to him. Yet, he'd tossed countless of them to girls in the front row of dives where he played. He'd probably lost more than that. A tiny piece of stiff plastic, a triangle with rounded corners, probably mass-produced in China or Bangladesh or God knows where.

He grunted softly. The tiny thing was so prevalent in his life and had been for some time, but he didn't know where they were made. Like the days of his life, so many had come and gone without notice. Now he was down to just one. All the others were just guitar picks, but this was his *last* guitar pick.

He sighed, fighting back his emotions. Part of him didn't want to believe the situation he was in. He still couldn't wrap his head around the shit Leopold was trying to explain to them. Infinite realities, infinite Benjamin Howards, all living different lives. It sounded like a science fiction movie. Add some ray guns and men in silver suits, and it'd be spot on for the "B" movies he used to watch as a kid.

But this wasn't science fiction. That much was sure. He'd

seen the world stop, watched Leopold appear and disappear. He remembered starting the same day over so many times.

Rubbing his face, he recalled Leopold's words as they stood amid the still traffic. "You're only hurting Angie," he'd said. "This Angie Howard can never move forward. Like you, her reality stops with the rest of the strand."

In the end, that had given him the strength to go through with it. He'd do what he had to do. For her. Leopold said she'd struggle for a bit, but then things would be okay. He said she'd meet someone who made her life better, someone who'd help her move on. Leopold assured him that she'd have a long and rewarding life.

Bennie drew in a deep breath, hoping that if some other guy was going to be banging his wife, he'd at least be rich. That way, she wouldn't have to work so hard. Hell, maybe she could even go to part-time.

Dropping his foot to the floor, Bennie sat up on the couch. He looked at the pick in his hand and shook his head. He was beginning the outro, the end of his song. He wouldn't be needing the pic anymore. Soon the music would fade, and he'd be gone.

He lifted his hand and thumbed the pick, watching it tumble through the dim light. It turned end over end as it flew across the room. Finally, it landed flat on the kitchen table and slid to a stop. Shaking his head, he laughed, knowing that he couldn't have landed the pick there if he tried.

"Must be my lucky day," he said sarcastically as he stood. He spared the pick one last look before heading back to the bedroom and his sleeping wife. He only had a few hours left and was going to make the most of them.

# CHAPTER TWENTY-ONE

"What?" Angie asked through an embarrassed chuckle.

"Nothing," Bennie answered with a wide smile.

"Why are you looking at me like that?"

"Like what?"

"Like a schoolboy who just got laid for the first time."

Bennie shrugged, his eyes shifting past his wife to the trio of women walking into the hospital. One of them wore the same color scrubs as Angie. The other two wore a light blue set.

"I guess I just enjoyed last night."

"You mean this morning?" she said, poking his ribs playfully.

"It was really nice." Bennie nodded. "And not just the sex. Everything. It was a nice thing to remember."

"What?" she asked, her brow wrinkling.

"Nothing." Bennie reached out a hand and cupped the back of Angie's neck. "I love you."

"I love you too." Angie leaned in and kissed him. "And it was awesome. I feel like a new woman." She arched her back and stretched. "Unfortunately, I have the same old job, though." She glanced at her watch. "I've got to go."

"You've already missed the danishes," Bennie quipped with a smile.

"That's fine. I'd rather have the time with you."

Bennie's heart sank. When Angie got out of the car, her time with him would be over. Clinging to Leopold's promise that she'd be okay, he forced a smile.

"But I do have to go."

Bennie watched his wife check her pockets, making sure she had the things she needed. When her inventory was over, he leaned in and pressed his lips to hers.

Angie moaned, enjoying the passion in Bennie's kiss. With all the stress they'd both been under lately, their intimacy had taken a nosedive.

"I wish we could stay here forever," Bennie said, staring into Angie's eyes as he pulled back from her.

"I know, babe. I have to clock in, and you've got that interview." She used a thumb to wipe the corner of Bennie's mouth. "But we can pick up where we left off this evening."

"I'd love that more than you know."

Angie rolled her eyes and smiled. "Okay, Romeo. Love you, babe." She opened the car door, leaned back in for a quick kiss, then bounded from the car.

Bennie watched her until the pneumatic doors closed behind her. When she was gone, he took a deep breath and melted into the seat.

How long would it be before she got the news? Would someone just call, or would a policeman show up like they did on television? Would they take her into one of those "family conference" rooms, or would they tell her right there at her station?

Bennie took a deep breath, pushing the images from his mind. If he didn't stop thinking about the aftermath, he wouldn't go through with the plan. He knew now that Leopold was right. Although he still couldn't wrap his head around all the science stuff, he remembered enough to know that they'd lived this same day more times than he could count. He also knew that nothing would ever change. They were stuck in some kind of loop, and there was only one way out.

When a horn beeped behind him, Bennie looked in the mirror. "Chill out, lady. You have more time than I do." Shaking his head, he put the car in gear and pulled away from the hospital.

———

Carver slid the knot in his tie up to his collar. Smiling, he smoothed it against the teal shirt he wore. Belinda had bought the set for him as a Christmas present, but he hadn't worn it yet.

"See," she said, tiptoeing to look over his shoulder, finding his eyes in the mirror. "I told you it would look nice."

Carver's eyes met hers, and his smile widened. "You did. And you were right."

"Do you really like the tie?" she asked, turning him to face her. "I know it's a little whimsical."

"I think it's perfect, just like you." His hands found her hips and pulled her to him.

Belinda rolled her eyes. "You'd think last night was our first time," she said, pulling the tie through her fingers. Her eyes washed over the yellow fabric, dotted with tiny fish that matched the shirt, then moved upwards suddenly, meeting his. Her brow creased deeply.

"Is everything okay?" she asked.

"Right as rain," Carver lied.

Belinda shook as a shudder ran through her. "I just had this odd feeling wash over me."

"Still weak in the knees?" Carver asked with a grin.

"I'm serious. Are you feeling okay?" She laid two fingers along his neck, taking his pulse.

"Stop," Carver said, taking her hands in his. "Everything's fine. Do you think I'm going to have a heart attack because we got busy? I'm not that old," he said with a laugh.

Belinda shrugged. "I don't know. I don't like this feeling. Maybe you should stay home."

"Sweetie, look at me. Today is just like every other day. I'm fine."

Belinda conceded with a sigh. "You know I always follow my gut on things like this."

*Always follow your gut, Carver.*

Carver smiled. "You know, my mother used to say the same thing."

"Smart woman," Belinda said, finally smiling.

Carver pulled her to him and held her tight. The faint scent of sweat mingled with the flowery smell of shampoo in her hair. When her body relaxed against him, he smiled.

Leopold had promised that she'd be okay, that she'd meet someone. Without that assurance, Carver wasn't sure he could go through with things. She had no future with him, but she had a future to live, and she was going to be okay. That's all that mattered now.

———

Things looked different to Bennie somehow. Admittedly, he wasn't used to the morning commute, but he recognized Leopold's hand in things he'd barely noticed before. Cars changed lanes for no reason, moving out of his way. Traffic lights stayed green longer than normal or changed to red unexpectedly. The latest of which had caught him and a group of other drivers at the last moment.

When he looked around, the man in the pickup next to him threw his hands up, looking at Bennie with a bewildered look on his face. Bennie shrugged, though he knew exactly what was going on.

Stroking his chin, Bennie stared out the windshield, wondering what Angie would do next week. Next year. He'd gathered all his equipment together to make it easier for her to sell, but he thought she'd hold onto it for a while. At least his guitar, anyway.

He did have a small term-life policy. Twenty-five grand. He'd bought it from a door-to-door guy in a cheap suit ten years ago. The guy was sweating buckets in the summer heat, and he felt sorry for him. It was only eight bucks a month. At least she wouldn't have to beg her father for the money to bury him.

As the light turned green and he moved forward, Bennie hoped Angie hadn't cashed it in. She hadn't said anything about it, but times were tough.

Moving with traffic, he began to wonder if Angie would sue Carver's estate. The guy was a lawyer; he had to be loaded. After all, he *did* run the light. That would make things easier for her. Maybe she'd get a fat settlement and wouldn't have to date some jobless loser.

*Like you?*

Bennie winced at his own thought. Emotional attachment aside, she'd be better off without him anyway. Honestly, what had he contributed to their marriage? To society, for that matter? He was just a down-and-out musician, like thousands of others around the world.

*Yet here you are, basically saving the world.*

A sad smile slipped across his lips. No one would ever know what he and Carver were about to do, but that wouldn't diminish their sacrifice. For whatever reason, this was supposed to happen, and they weren't going to run from it anymore.

Bennie picked up the phone in the passenger seat. His eyes traced the thin blue line to its end at the intersection of Main Avenue and 14th Street. That was where it all began and where it would all end.

The abrupt stop of his route sent his heart racing. Panic gripped his chest. He took a deep breath and blew it out slowly, but it didn't help. Suddenly, the weight of what he was about to do felt too big. Too heavy. He was going to die. Benjamin Howard would cease to exist.

"God," he said aloud. "I don't even know if you're listening to me. I mean, I haven't been to church in years, and that was only because my mama made me go. And God, I mean, you know I haven't been what you'd call a choir boy either."

Bennie sighed and pushed a hand over his sweaty brow. He looked around at the other drivers. A middle-aged woman with short brown hair was looking at him, wide-eyed. He offered her a wave, and she looked away.

"I guess I don't even know what to say. I don't want

anything for me. Except maybe to let it be quick. I think it will be, you know. But help Ange out, if it's not too much trouble. She's no angel either, but she's a good woman."

Bennie rubbed his face. He felt like a hypocrite, asking for favors at the last minute. He'd never put much stock in organized religion, but figured it couldn't hurt. He had no choice but to trust Leopold, but he wasn't sure how far his powers or willingness would go. What was it that Carver had said? Or was it Leopold?

Something about there being no atheists in hell. Either way, it never hurt to hedge your bets.

———

Carver stared at the rusty patch on the tailgate of the truck in front of him, thinking that he must be ahead of schedule. True to form, the old man was meandering along at fifty-five miles per hour. Though he wasn't riding his bumper this morning, Carver noticed the guy looking back at him several times.

He chuckled, wondering how badly the old man was cursing him. He guessed plenty. Every time he saw the guy, he'd get nothing but an angry stare, as if he resented being passed.

When the truck rolled to a stop at the end of Highway Eleven, the line of traffic was long, but no one seemed to be in a big hurry. Carver sighed and settled into his seat, sure that he'd be where he needed to be when the time was right.

Watching the guy's rearview mirror through his back glass, he caught the old man's eyes. Carver offered a smile but didn't get one in return. He couldn't undo years of tailgating in one morning. Or could he?

His eyes went to the money bag on the seat next to him. When he'd grabbed it on his way out the door, he wasn't sure why. Now, an idea was beginning to tickle the back of his mind. Could he give the cash to the old man? Would Leo allow it?

Carver rubbed his chin and checked the oncoming traffic. The first group had passed, but another was coming. He knew from experience that the old man wouldn't go until the road was completely clear as far as he could see. If he went now, he could make it. If Leopold didn't like it, he could take care of it himself.

"What the hell?" Carver grabbed the money bag and opened his door. When he started for the truck, he saw the old man's eyes trained on him in the side-view mirror.

"Hey there," Carver said, offering a smile and a wave as he approached the open window on the driver's side. "Good morning."

The old man stared back at Carver but said nothing.

Carver extended a hand. "I'm Carver Willis."

"I know who you are. You're that hotshot lawyer with all them commercials on the television."

Carver nodded. "Guilty as charged," he said with a chuckle. When the old man didn't laugh, Carver cleared his throat. "Look, anyway, I figure that I've passed you a hundred times."

"'Bout right. I'm surprised you ain't wrecked and killed yourself by now."

"You're more right about that than you know." When a gray minivan pulled up behind his car, Carver offered them a wave and then turned back to the old man.

"You headed to work or something?"

"If it's any of your business, I'm headed up to the nursing home to feed my wife breakfast."

Carver nodded. "Anyway, look." He pulled the money bag to his chest and patted it. "I just want to apologize for being such an asshole all these mornings. I mean, I didn't know…"

The old man's eyes narrowed. "All right then. I best be going."

"Wait. Wait." Carver held the bag out to the man. "I want you to have this."

"What is it?"

"Money. Twenty-seven grand, to be exact."

The old man's eyes bulged, his thin eyebrows rising

onto his forehead. "Holy hell. That's a lot of money. You done embezzle it or something?"

Carver chuckled. "Not a cent of it."

The old man leaned out the window, eyeing Carver suspiciously. "Are you sick in the head or something?"

"No. I—" When the minivan honked, Carver waved them around. "Look, mister, it's all legit. The way I figure it, we've all got to pay for the crap we dish out. I don't have time to go around town making amends, so I'm just going to do it all in one lump."

"By giving me a sack of money?"

"Exactly." Carver held the bag out again.

"All the same," the man said with a curt nod of his head. "But I have to go."

"Don't you want it?" Carver asked, extending the bag to the man.

"I'll tell you what. My Mavis was sick for a long time before she went into the home. Cancer, you know."

Carver nodded, but he didn't know shit about the man in front of him except that he drove slow and always looked angry.

"I worked thirty years at the plant and retired. Ended up losing the house when she got put in that place. It's a shit hole, but it's all we can get. That's why I go and feed her breakfast." When the car that had pulled up behind Carver honked, the old man extended a boney arm and waved him around.

"I live in a back room at my daughter's house, and her two kids are about as big a brats as I bet you ever seen. I mostly keep to myself and sit and talk to Mavis, though lately, I wonder if she even knows who I am."

Carver looked into the old man's tired, weepy eyes and felt his pain and loneliness. He shoved the bag through the window. "Man, I wish it were more. I really do." Carver turned to leave, but the man stopped him.

"You wanna know what I'm going to do with this money?"

"It's none of my business."

The man's face lit up. "I'm gonna get Mavis and just drive out west. She's always wanted to see the Grand Canyon, and maybe that big ole dam they got out there."

"That sounds like a great idea." Carver sidestepped a car as it rolled past, the driver staring darts at him. "I really have to be going." Carver looked at his watch. Leopold was going to have to work to get him there on time as it was.

"They probably won't allow it, though," the man continued. "Damned doctors."

Carver absorbed the man's sorrow like a gut punch. "You said you've seen my commercials? Call my office and ask to speak to Jean. Tell her what you want to do with your wife and that I told you 'Goldilocks'."

"Like the three bears?"

"Exactly. She'll know what it means. My office will take care of any legal issues for you regarding your wife, pro bono."

"Does that mean free?"

"It sure does. Anyway, sorry to rush, but I got an appointment that I can't miss." He threw the man a wave and hurried back to his Mercedes. "Goldilocks" was the codeword that they shared in the office when someone really wanted something; when the case was just right.

———

Settling into his seat, Carver chuckled. "The Old Man", whose name he still didn't know, had pulled off from the stop sign and was headed toward town. He'd have to pass him one more time.

The black Mercedes barely slowed at the intersection, the road to his left clear as far as he could see. He gunned the gas and sped onto the highway, catching the old pickup quickly. Slipping into the oncoming lane, Carver smiled. His car glided gently up to the truck. As he drew even, the old man smiled and gave him a nod. Carver gave him a salute and then sped past, easing into the lane ahead of the truck. He offered a quick wave and pressed the gas pedal.

# CHAPTER TWENTY-TWO

Bennie wiped the sweat from his brow as he waited at the traffic light. The same old utility work had snarled traffic, but he there was no sign of the guy smoking. Of course, it was Leopold, and now that they were both committed to the plan, he hadn't made an appearance.

He'd seen a lot of the same people. The cute blonde and her muscle-bound driver, the old woman who'd once flipped him off. They were all there like any other day, which, for them, it was.

Bennie's eyes shifted to the traffic passing through the intersection before him. People were headed to work, probably thinking about the day ahead of them. He wondered how many of them were making plans for after work. Supper at home. Maybe drinks with a co-worker.

Sadness welled in his chest again, and he took a deep breath to combat it. He only had a matter of minutes to live. What would he do with the precious little time he had left?

He switched on the radio and tuned it to the local rock station, WSHK, shock radio. The DJ was rambling on about his commute.

"C'mon, man," Bennie moaned. He wanted to go out to a kick-ass song, not some guy bitching about his drive-in. "Leopold, please."

On the radio, the DJ fell silent for a moment, then said, "But enough about that. Who's ready to rock?"

When the opening chords to Metallica's "Enter Sandman" filtered through the speaker, Bennie smiled. "Hell yeah! Thanks, dude." He turned the volume up as far as it would go and let the thundering sounds of guitars wash over him.

He looked to his left, waiting. Soon, the opposing traffic light would turn yellow, and traffic would begin to slow. Then a big black Mercedes would come barreling down the road.

*If the truth means that it's over…Then please, baby, tell me lies. 'Cause I'm stuck here in a prison… where dreams go to die. I might be losing my mind. I might be going crazy. Or just waiting for death to come…in a big black Mercedes.*

Bennie took a deep breath and let it out slowly while he waited for the light. He wiped one sweaty palm on the leg of his jeans, then the other. The seconds passed by with agonizing slowness. At this point, he just wanted it to be over.

He watched the shift in traffic as it happened. Cars approaching the light sped up while those behind them slowed. When a blue two-door car darted past, the coast was clear. He didn't bother looking up at the light but rolled into the intersection.

His hand went to his seatbelt, and he considered taking it off, then reconsidered. Not wearing it might affect the meager life insurance policy he had. Besides, he'd worn it every other time.

His heart was thundering as loud as the bass on the radio. He was down to seconds now. He swallowed hard and then saw the grill of the black Mercedes suddenly appear from behind an ancient yellow Impala. The morning sun glinted off the shiny chrome.

He drew in a deep breath and clenched his body, preparing for the impact.

———

Carver found himself amazed at the scope of Leopold's reach. This morning's commute had been a dream. Fourteen was almost deserted, and he was able to easily pass the few cars he'd encountered.

The sky was a beautiful, cloudless, blue, and the soothing sound of Brian Sandel's voice was in rare form. The Mercedes purred beneath him like a contented cat, responding to his every command flawlessly. He even had to admit to himself that the fabric of the shirt Belinda had bought felt much better than the rough fabric of his other shirts.

Any other time, he'd proclaim it a perfect morning, but today was different. Today, he'd go away. Carver Willis would be no more. The thought hurt, but also didn't at the same time. What he felt was something akin to the satisfaction of completing an important case, and getting into bed after a long, frustrating day rolled into one emotion.

He thought again of the old man, hoping that Leopold would allow him to keep the money and that it brought both him and his wife some joy. He'd seen the man so many times, never knowing that he was going to feed his ailing wife breakfast. He'd thought him just an angry old man, and maybe he was. But he had good reason to be angry. Losing everything he'd worked for just because his wife was sick. That would make any man angry.

As he entered the flyover, Carver peeked over the concrete wall lining the bridge. Treetops gave way to a wide, slow-moving river. A lone boat was headed upriver, leaving a white wake in the dark water. He'd never been much of a fisherman but always meant to buy a pontoon boat. He'd always heard that guys who had boats got laid a lot more than guys who didn't. Of course, that was before Belinda. Since he'd met her, he'd gotten lucky as often as he could stand.

Carver wasn't aware that he was smiling until the thought of Belinda erased it from his face. He hated knowing that she'd be hurt because of what would happen. Her feelings for him were genuine, and though she never brought it up, he was sure she hoped they'd marry.

Carver shook his head, regretting not marrying her. How might that have changed things on this strand? Maybe they would buy a different house and a different commute. Maybe he'd work from home more, slow down, and enjoy some of the money he'd made.

He sighed, remembering that Leopold had said that regret

was a waste of time. He was right, but it didn't help. Carver knew his end was rapidly approaching and wished he'd done things differently. He should have a wife and kids by now. Maybe be coaching little league baseball or something, taking the little guy to the park, or teaching him how to tie a tie. He should have, but he didn't. And now his time was up.

The Mercedes slipped beneath the green light at the edge of town. Looking ahead, Carver saw that all the lights were green. He'd wasted time talking to the old man, and now Leopold was having to work hard to get him there on time. Carver depressed the gas pedal and slipped into the next lane, passing a big black pickup truck.

He made the second light with ease. One block away. His eyes washed over traffic, mapping his path. He moved into the right lane as the car in front of him slowed. He spared a glance at the young woman as he passed her red car. There was a peaceful glow on her face, lending Carver a smile.

His eyes came back to the road in time to see Bennie's silver Camry roll to a stop in the intersection. He was waiting for him.

Carver blew past a white SUV as it stopped for the red light. Bennie was staring at him, watching him approach. The smile on his face looked forced.

Carver's foot wanted to lift from the accelerator, but he wouldn't let it. He drew in a deep breath and steered directly for Bennie. They had to get this right this time.

As the Mercedes passed under the light, Carver returned Bennie's smile. His was forced and he knew it. He gasped as a mixture of fear and panic washed through him, but he gripped the wheel hard and closed his eyes.

# CHAPTER TWENTY-THREE

The sound of the crash echoed through the downtown district, drawing the attention of people blocks away. A flock of red-winged blackbirds took flight from a tree, squawking loudly.

A crowd began to form immediately, pointing and gawking at the horrific collision. The impact pushed both cars through the intersection. They ended up as one mangled heap blocking the left three lanes of Main Avenue.

On 14th Street, a blonde woman got out of a white Yukon. She took one step toward the crash site, then stopped. Her hand went to her mouth as she stared at the scene in disbelief. A well-muscled man in a tank top joined her at the front of their vehicle.

A man in a dark blue service uniform rushed to the cars, looking to render aid. He took one look inside the mangled black Mercedes and realized that there was none to give. A stocky man with gray hair joined him at the window, then turned from Carver's destroyed car, waving his hands for people to stay back.

Most of the crowd did just that, fearing an explosion. Diagonally across the intersection, a young man pulled his sporty red car to the curb and got out. He joined an older man and two women on the street discussing what they'd just witnessed. The older man mentioned how fast the Mercedes was going. The young man said that it looked like the silver car had stopped in the intersection.

A young woman, one hand resting on her swollen belly, clambered from her car, obviously shaken. On the street just beyond her car, the driver of the antique Impala got down on his knees right there on the asphalt and began to pray.

On the sidewalk near the mangled cars, Leopold stood with his suit coat hanging over his right shoulder. His eyes were locked on the mangled heaps of metal. He didn't need to see inside to know that both men were dead. The fact that the strand hadn't stopped told him that it was over, but it was a bittersweet moment.

He'd spent more time with the two men occupying the cars in front of him than he had with anyone else since becoming a Keeper. He'd gotten to know their lives intimately, spoken to them so many times, that he almost felt like his old self again. Now that he'd succeeded in setting things right, he'd go back to being unseen, unnoticed. To not talking to people. He'd once again be invisible to the world he kept.

Leopold released a heavy sigh and thanked the men, sparing them one last look before turning and moving away. Walking along the sidewalk with one hand in his pocket and his head down, he didn't look up when the police car raced past him, lights and sirens blaring. The police were going toward the wreck, he was walking away from it.

Suddenly, he needed to go to the garden and immerse himself in the beauty of the place, to find his peace again.

# CHAPTER TWENTY-FOUR

Angie Howard swept her eyes across the park. The first warm Saturday of spring had brought people out of hiding. The sun was shining, the rich blue sky seemed to go on forever. It had been a long, cold winter, and she was glad to feel the sun on her back.

She looked over the fifty or so kids playing on the equipment. The sounds of their laughter brought a smile to her lips. The parents, mostly women though some men were scattered about, sat on the fringes of the play area, like her. Most of them were chatting with other parents, presumably tag-alongs for a play date.

She found one man pushing his son on the swing. They were both laughing. She sighed heavily and looked away, her eyes going misty. In the sandbox thirty feet from the bench she occupied, a thin, sandy-haired boy played alone. A sad smile came to her lips, and her heart broke a little.

She'd raised her son alone for five years but had enjoyed every minute of it. Physically, he was built like she'd imagined Bennie had been as a child. He was a little on the small side but had a big heart. The doctors hadn't pinned down exactly where he was on the spectrum yet, but it didn't matter. He was hers, and every ounce of her loved him dearly.

Her brow furrowed, and her chest tightened as another kid approached the sandbox. The kid was twice Ben's size, and the look on his face wasn't friendly. She stood slowly, watching the scene intently.

When the kid stepped on Ben's sandcastle, she started toward him. The kid was looking down at Ben. He said something, then laughed. Her son was staring up at the kid in disbelief, but made no attempt to stand.

As Angie hastened her pace, movement out of the corner of her eye caught her attention. To her left, not far from the sandbox, a boy leaped from the swing and landed deftly on his feet. He was a thickly built kid, but still moved faster than her, racing toward the sandbox. Hopping the short wall that kept the sand contained, he lunged at the kid standing over Ben. Both hands landed on the boy's chest, sending him staggering back. His arms flailed, and he tripped over the far wall, landing onto his back outside the sandbox.

The mother, who was hovering close enough to protect her own child but not close enough to prevent his bullying, swooped in. She arrived seconds before Angie.

"What's wrong with you?" she asked, staring at the boy who'd shoved her son. "That was uncalled for," she complained, helping her son up and brushing dirt from the back of his sweatshirt.

"I could ask your kid the same thing," Angie said as she arrived, kneeling next to Ben. "Your son was the aggressor here in case you missed it."

The woman, dressed in a matching jogging suit, scoffed. "C'mon, son, let's get away from these people."

Angie looked up at the kid standing beside Ben. He was stocky and had a head full of black hair. His brow was slightly furrowed as if he were trying to figure something out.

"Thank you," she said, smiling.

The boy shrugged and turned to leave, but his mother showed up. She was older and heavier than Angie, her face painted with concern. She put one protective hand around the boy's shoulder and raked her blonde bangs from her face with the other.

"Hey, buddy," she said, breathing heavily. "What's going on?"

"He's fine," Angie said with a warm smile. "That other

kid was being…a jerk." She looked at the boy again. "Your son just put him in his place."

"Still." Belinda turned her son to face her. "You can't just go around pushing kids over. Okay? He could have been hurt, sweetie."

The boy shrugged again. "We don't have to leave, do we? I'm sorry."

The woman shrugged, sparing a glance at the mother and her son as they walked toward the parking lot. "No, I guess not. But you have to play nice."

"Okay, Mama."

Angie stood, watching as the boy kneeled in the sandbox. "You good?" she asked Ben. Busy packing sand into a small yellow bucket, his reply was one curt nod.

Angie sighed and brushed sand from the knee of her jeans. "Please don't be upset with your son. Honestly, he's kinda my hero right now."

The blonde smiled as she joined Angie outside of the sandbox. "He's a big kid, and sometimes he doesn't realize it. We've had some issues in pre-school."

Angie looked back at the boys. Watching them play together, she smiled. Ben's condition made it hard for him to make friends, and the sight warmed her heart. As she watched, he lifted the upturned bucket of sand. When the sand didn't release, he banged it on the ground. When he lifted it again, the sand tumbled out in clumps.

"Almost. Keep trying, sweetie. You'll get it." She turned to the blond. "Sorry. I'm Angie Howard," she said, extending a hand.

"Belinda. Belinda Marcum." She shook the slender hand extended to her. "That bundle of energy is Carver."

Angie bent at the waist. "Well, Ben doesn't talk a lot, so I'll say it for him. Thank you, Carver Marcum. You're my hero."

"That's not my name," the boy said, sparing Angie a

quizzical look and a laugh.

"I'm sorry," Belinda said. "He has his father's name. Willis."

Angie's face went pale as she stared at the woman in front of her. In her mind, she put the names together, and her heart stopped. "Carver Willis?"

"Yeah," Belinda said, her concern growing. "Are you okay?"

Angie rubbed her face with both hands and then shoved them through her hair. "You don't know who I am. Do you?"

"Should I?"

Angie speared the kids a look, then took Belinda by the elbow. She led her to a deserted balance beam and sat down. "I'm Angie Howard. My husband's name is Benjamin Howard. Or rather... it was."

It was Belinda's turn to gasp. She'd read the newspaper clippings surrounding the accident enough times to memorize them. So many nights she'd lain in bed, unable to fight back tears, and thought of the people behind the names. Benjamin Howard. Angie Howard. She often wondered if, somewhere across town, another woman was doing the same. She wondered if Benjamin Howard's wife was cursing Carver's name, his existence on this earth.

As the pain faded with time, she sometimes wondered if that woman was piecing her life back together. She wondered if her face was among the strangers she saw in the grocery store, if they'd unknowingly shared an elevator.

"Is Ben's father...?"

Angie nodded, her face taking on the shroud of sadness. "That's the one."

Belinda's knees went weak, and she sat down hard on the beam next to Angie. Leaning forward, she rested her elbows on her knees and covered her face with her hands. "All this time..."

The woman beside her was a ghost, real, but not. The

possibility of meeting her someday, of having to face the woman whose husband Carver had killed, haunted her. She'd had dreams of meeting her, tears streaming down her face. Angry. Shouting. Blaming Carver and her.

"I never knew y'all had a kid."

"Same here. I guess with all the shock and then the pregnancy..." Angie shook her head.

Belinda moaned through her hands. "I've actually had nightmares about this day. Meeting you, I mean." She moaned again as she dropped her hands. Her eyes watched as she nervously picked at a fingernail. "Do you hate me?"

"What?" Angie asked with a confused chuckle. "Why would I hate you?"

Belinda sat up. "Ben's father ran that red light. It was his fault. It's all in the police report. Surely you've read them a thousand times like I have. I'm so sorry."

Angie put a hand on Belinda's back. "Oh, I did. Believe me. Different witnesses said different things. Neither of us really knows what happened. Maybe nobody does." She looked at her son and smiled. "Look, I've made peace with all that. I had to, for his sake."

"Yeah." Belinda shook her head. "Can I tell you something?"

Angie shrugged, her eyes going to the kids. "Sure."

"We weren't married, but we were together that last night. Carver was different. I can't explain it. In hindsight, I almost want to think he knew something was going to happen, like he knew he wasn't coming home."

Angie's brow creased as she thought. A sad smile slipped across her lips, and she nodded slowly. "As crazy as it sounds, I've thought the same thing. It's weird. I just thought that, in my mind, I was just making that last night together more than it was. We were like kids again, you know. Lying in bed, laughing, holding each other. It's like when we first started dating."

Belinda shook her head. "They couldn't have known. Could they?"

Angie shook her head. "No way. I mean, Bennie wouldn't have even been there if not for a job interview." She pushed a hand through her hair as she fought a pang of guilt. "Besides, if they somehow knew, surely they'd avoid it."

Belinda nodded. "That makes sense, but..."

"Honestly, I try to avoid thinking about that day. The doctors said it was quick, you know. That neither of them suffered. I'm thankful for that."

Belinda nodded as she watched her son, Carver's son, play in the sand.

Angie put a hand on Belinda's shoulder. "I'm not going to say it hasn't been hard, but I've learned that you can't do anything to change the past. I've tried to look to the future, especially with Ben. You asked if I hated you; the answer's no. I don't even hate your husband."

"Oh, thank God." Belinda looked at the two boys playing in the sand. "What a hell of a thing to have happen, to both of them." She nodded toward Ben, trying to figure out his age. The boy was thin and small compared to her son. "How old was he when it happened?"

Angie shook her head. "I was pregnant."

"Did your husband know?"

Angie shook her head again. "I didn't even know."

"Me either," Belinda said with a gasp. She pushed her hand through her hair. "Ben's father and I weren't married. That's why our names are different. I wanted him to have his father's name."

Angie nodded, her gaze going to the boys. Ben was squatting, his sneakers buried in the sand. He patted the full bucket of dirt with the palm of his hand, packing it in the bucket.

"You gotta flip it fast," Carver explained, helping Ben flip the bucket. "Now, you have to tap it. Like this, see?" He rapped on the bottom of the bucket with his knuckles.

Angie held her breath as Ben slowly lifted the bucket, revealing the molded sand. When both boys cheered, she smiled.

"Ben is on the spectrum," Angie explained. "Kids can be mean, you know. He has trouble making friends."

"Well, looks like he's made one now."

Angie nodded, her smile widening. "Do you guys come to this park a lot?"

Belinda nodded. "Oh yeah, when the weather allows. I have to let that one run some energy out or he'll be bouncing off the walls all evening."

"We do too," Angie said, watching the boys play. She closed her eyes and took a deep breath. "You know, it was hard for a long time. I mean, the accident and then finding out that I was pregnant." She shook her head. "Then knowing he'd never know his father."

"I know. I was lost until I found out I was pregnant. After that, I knew my mission in life was to raise that kid the best I could."

Angie nodded. "It's strange that we haven't met each other before now." She allowed her eyes to sweep over the other kids playing, wondering how many times she'd accidentally crossed paths with Belinda and her son without knowing it.

It would have been easy to miss them. When they came to the park, most of her attention was on Ben. He wasn't like the other kids. She couldn't just relax and gossip with the other mothers. She had to watch him every second.

Belinda smiled as she watched the boys pack the bucket with sand again. "Maybe the time just wasn't right until now."

Angie nodded and smiled, watching both boys gently raise the bucket to reveal another perfect mold of sand. "I think maybe you're right."

John Ryland lives and writes in Northport, Alabama, with his wife and two sons. His previous works include the novels *Souls Harbor* and *Shatter*, the collection of short stories entitled *Southern Gothic*, and a poetry chapbook, *The Stranger, Poems from the Chair*. You can find his other works in publications such *as Bewildering Stories, The Eldritch Journal, The Writer's Magazine, Otherwise Engaged, The Birmingham Arts Journal, Subterranean Blue,* and others, as well as the online journal *The Chamber Magazine*. His novel *The Man with No Eyes* was released in March 2022.

When not writing or attending various sporting events for his sons, he enjoys gardening, people-watching, and wondering what makes people do the things they do.